MISCHIEF IN MONTANA

MONTANA SWEET WESTERN CONTEMPORARY ROMANCE SERIES

PAMELA M. KELLEY

UNTITLED

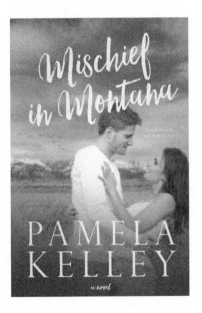

UNTITLED

MISCHIEF IN MONTANA
By
Pamela M. Kelley
Piping Plover Press
Copyright 2014, Pamela M. Kelley
All rights reserved
Edited by Cindy Tahse
Cover design by Sarah Hansen, Okay Designs
ISBN 978-1-953060-08-2

If you'd like to receive my new release alerts, special promos, giveaways and early release discounts, sign up for my mailing list, http://eepurl.com/IZbOH

CHAPTER 1

What do you think about this one?" Isabella Graham turned slowly so her Uncle Jim and her sister, Jen, could see the full effect of the dress. They had been waiting patiently in her kitchen while she tried on different dresses for their approval.

"I don't know much about these things, but isn't there some rule about not wearing white because of the bride?" Uncle Jim, who was usually smiling and happy, sat just shaking his head.

"It's not white, it's cream. Still too close?" The dress was beautiful and new. Isabella had just discovered it a week ago at a tiny shop in Bozeman, and had fallen in love, instantly. It was the kind of love that happened to her often, as she was a bit of a clothes-a-holic and frequently engaged in 'retail therapy', as she put it.

"It's gorgeous, but you need to blend in more, not draw attention. It's Traci's day," Jen reminded her.

Isabella sighed. "I know, but I just love this dress."

"Well, you have fifty million others. Go try again, and hurry up, will ya? We don't want to be late." Uncle Jim was teasing her now and Isabella glanced at the clock. They needed to leave in less than ten minutes.

"What about my red one? You were with me when I bought that one, remember?" she asked Jen.

"Yes, and it's an absolute no. That will make you stand out even more than the cream. What about something softer? Did I remember seeing a pretty yellow dress in your closet? I don't think I've ever seen you wear that."

Isabella thought for a minute. "I bought that one a year ago and have worn it a few times, but not in months. That could work."

A few minutes later, she came back downstairs and both Uncle Jim and Jen gave their approvals. It was a flattering dress, made of a soft, floaty fabric and had a draped boatneck with three-quarter length sleeves. The pale yellow made her long, dark brown hair look almost black and the clever cut of the design hid the five pounds around her middle that she was forever trying to lose.

Her sister, Jen, who was just two years younger, looked great in her dress, too, which was long and flowing and in a dusty rose shade that brought out the deep, red highlights in her chestnut brown hair. Their shared date for the wedding was Uncle Jim. He was actually their father's uncle and was more like a grandfather to both girls as he was in his early nineties. They adored him, and he loved to spend time with 'his girls', as he often called them. They were meeting her parents at the church and had to be there extra early as Jen was in the wedding, as her best friend, Traci's, maid of honor.

When they arrived at the church, Jen ran off to finish getting ready with the wedding party, and Isabella and Uncle Jim decided to take a stroll through the church gardens. It was a beautiful, warm summer afternoon, and the sun was shining. The gardens were gorgeous, full of bright flowers that sent the most wonderful smells their way as the breeze softly blew around them.

"Let's sit a spell," Uncle Jim said as they approached an ornate, wrought-iron bench that was painted white.

"How's business?" he asked Isabella as they settled themselves on the not very comfortable bench.

"It's great! I closed on two big deals this week and have a new buyer looking for a ranch, which could be another really big one. I'm on track to be the top broker again this month. That would make four months in a row." Isabella sold real estate. She loved her work and was very good at it.

"I'm proud of you, honey. That's really great." Uncle Jim looked thoughtful for a moment. "I hear that Missy Atwell is going to be joining your firm."

"Melissa Atwell? I thought she was an elementary school teacher." Isabella couldn't see it. Melissa was a somewhat mousy and timid type. She was also very sweet and well-liked around town, but a real estate agent?

"Her grandfather tells me she just got her real estate license. Said she's ready to try something new."

"Well, good luck to her. It's very different from teaching, I can't imagine she'll like it. People tend to think it's a lot easier than it is. Sales is hard." Isabella did wish her well, though. Melissa was a nice person, and she wasn't likely to be any kind of a threat to Isabella's business.

"Not everyone is as competitive as you are. I bet she'll do fine. People like to work with people they know and like."

Isabella frowned at that. It sounded a little bit like a dig and her Uncle Jim wasn't like that.

"What are you saying?"

"Just that I worry about you sometimes, sweetie. You know I love you to death, but you're so competitive. I know it's because you're really good at what you do and you're passionate about it, but some people might find that intimidating." He patted her knee and smiled. "Just loosen up a little is what I'm saying. Try and relax more and enjoy the moment."

Isabella was stunned into silence, and a little hurt. She knew that Uncle Jim was just trying to be helpful, though, and didn't have a mean bone in his body. He truly just wanted everyone to be as happy as he was. After a minute, she smiled back and politely said, "I'll think about that. So, should we head in now?"

THE CHURCH WAS STARTING TO FILL UP AS THEY MADE THEIR way to the seats that Jen had saved for them. They were right up front, behind the wedding party and immediate family. Traci had been Jen's best friend for as long as Isabella could remember. It seemed to Isabella that Traci was getting married awfully quickly, as she and Dan, her fiance, had met less than six months ago. Dan was the brother of Isabella's ex-boyfriend, Christian, and he would never have even met Traci if he hadn't broken his leg and had to leave Chicago to recuperate at the family ranch in Beauville, Montana.

Though the six month time period had worked for Christian, too. To say that Isabella wasn't pleased when Christian abruptly broke things off with her while they were eating lunch one day was an understatement. Especially when he told her it was because he was going to marry someone else in two weeks. It seemed ridiculous even now as she thought about it, and at the time it was infuriating. It wasn't that she'd been madly in love with Christian, it was mostly that it looked bad. Everyone knew they'd been dating for months. But, although they enjoyed each other's company, if she was being truthful, she had to admit that there had never been a great passion there. Respect and admiration, sure, but butterflies? No.

It had seemed, at first, that his marriage truly was just for convenience. Christian's grandfather had played matchmaker in his will and added a condition that in order to inherit, Christian had to marry Molly, a woman who had lived in Beauville as a child. Molly left a promising career in Manhattan to marry Christian with the understanding that in six months, they could go their separate ways. But, Christian's grandfather was wise, and instead, they fell in love and stayed married. Now, his brother was about to tie the knot as well.

Meanwhile, Isabella was utterly single. However, she did have her sights set on someone. Aidan Summers, who she'd had such a crush on in high school, had just moved back home after many years away. He was a renowned artist, a painter of light-filled landscapes that had earned him a world-wide reputation. He traveled quite a bit, but rumor had it that he was tired of the lifestyle and was ready to settle down, possibly in Beauville.

Out of the corner of her eye, she caught a glimpse of pale, blonde hair and saw that it was Aidan, settling into a pew diagonally across from her. He even looked the part of an artist, with pale skin, blue eyes and hair so blonde that it was almost white. It just brushed his shoulders, which would be too long for most people, but the look suited him. An older woman sat next to him, his Aunt Edna. Isabella knew that he was staying with her and wondered if he had plans to get his own place. She could certainly help him there.

Moments later, the music started and all eyes went to the back of the church. Jennifer was the first bridesmaid to come down the aisle, followed soon after by Traci's cousin, Anne, then Molly, and finally, Traci and her father slowly made their way through the church. As she did at all weddings, Isabella felt her eyes water as she watched Traci, who looked so beautiful, and her father, who seemed both terrified and incredibly proud at the same time.

Waiting at the altar was Jeff, Dan's best friend from Chicago, Dan, of course, Christian, and Travis, Traci's brother. They all looked handsome in their charcoal black tuxes. Dan was positively beaming and couldn't take his eyes off Traci. Vows were exchanged and, in a flash, they were pronounced husband and wife.

Even Uncle Jim's eyes looked a bit misty as he turned to Isabella and said, "You ready to get out of here? Don't want to miss out on the snacks. I'm starving."

Isabella chuckled. "I'm ready. Oh, and I heard they're having one of your favorites, pigs-in-a-blanket," she said as they stood to make their way out of the church.

"Those little hot dogs? Excellent choice." Uncle Jim was funny; nothing made him happier than a hot dog.

Jen rode in the limo with the rest of the wedding party, and Isabella drove herself and Uncle Jim to the Knights of Columbus hall for the wedding reception.

When they walked inside, she found their place cards on a long table, and led Uncle Jim to their assigned seats. They were at a round banquet table that would seat ten people and were the first to arrive. Uncle Jim settled into his chair and Isabella went off to the bar to fetch drinks. She returned with a fruity Planter's Punch for Uncle Jim and a soda water and cranberry with a splash of lime for herself.

Once in a great while, Isabella had a glass of champagne or wine, but generally, she preferred not to drink. It wasn't that she didn't like alcohol or had a problem with it. She actually enjoyed the taste, but was concerned that it could become a problem someday as alcohol dependency ran in her family, so it was just easier to avoid it. Plus, although she did like the taste, she didn't like the way it made her feel. One of Isabella's biggest fears was losing control, and the easiest way to avoid that was to simply not drink.

Their table started to fill up moments after they arrived and it was a lively group. Molly's mother and Aunt Betty sat next to Uncle Jim, and Isabella was pleased to see that Aidan and his aunt were immediately to her left. Jen must have worked with Traci on the seating arrangements. His Aunt Edna settled into the seat next to Isabella and then she saw Missy Atwell and her brother, David, making their way towards the table. Missy sat next to Aidan, but Isabella wasn't concerned. She couldn't imagine that they'd have much in common. The final couple to join their table was Billy and his new girlfriend. Billy was Traci's ex-boyfriend and worked at the high school as a gym teacher and football coach. He'd met his girlfriend, Linda, there as she was a guidance counselor. She used to work at the elementary school before moving into guidance work, so she knew Missy well and they started chatting immediately and catching up.

Isabella hadn't had a chance to really talk to Aidan since he'd moved home, so was thrilled that they'd been seated at the same table. She waited until he glanced her way, and then asked, "So, I hear you might be back in town to stay for a while?"

"I just sold my co-op in Brooklyn last week and, fortunately, Aunt Edna agreed to put me up for a while. Until I figure out where to go from here." He smiled playfully at his aunt and her face lit up.

"I'm just thrilled to have him back, as you can imagine. I've told him he's welcome to stay with me as long as he'd like and I'm hoping he'll decide to move here permanently."

"I've always loved it here," he agreed.

"He was traveling so much," Aunt Edna added and Aidan made a face.

"Yeah, the travel part of the job was getting really old. It's an honor being invited to show my work, and at first it was exciting to visit different cities and countries. But, after a while, it gets to be a grind. I'm cutting way back."

"I imagine you can use the internet more now, to show your work?" Isabella wondered out loud.

"Yeah, absolutely. My manager has been great about finding ways to use the internet to market me."

"Are you going to show your pictures here in town, too?" Missy interjected and Aidan turned his attention her way.

"I might, if there's a gallery that would be interested."

"Oh, I'm sure there must be," Missy said and Isabella tried not to show her annoyance. She had to admit, Missy looked very pretty in her soft, lavender dress. It was the perfect color to highlight her blond hair that was a perfectly arranged tangle of shiny curls that just brushed her shoulders. She had big, blue eyes and a cute, turned-up nose that gave her a look of sexy innocence. It was a look that was very much her opposite and though Isabella had never suffered from a lack of male attention, she couldn't help but wonder what Aidan's type might be. He was a bit hard to read. He'd always been pleasant and friendly, flirtatious even, but never obviously interested, which made him that much more of a challenge.

During dinner everyone at the table chatted easily and had lots of questions for Aidan. As a famous artist, he was the closest thing Beauville had to a celebrity and everyone was curious about his plans. He didn't commit to anything, though, just that he was looking forward to relaxing and spending time with his aunt and catching up with old friends.

Once all the dishes had been cleared and the cake was cut and served, the band shifted gears and started playing dance music. Uncle Jim was one of the first ones on the dance floor and dragged Isabella along with him. She didn't mind, though. She loved to dance and Uncle Jim was an outstanding dancer. He could dance to anything. Jen bounced over to join them and Traci and Dan were right behind her, followed by Molly and Christian. The dance floor filled up quickly and soon almost everyone was up dancing and having a great time.

After a few fast songs, the music slowed and Isabella glanced around, looking for Aidan. She felt a tap on her shoulder and turned to see Travis Jones, Traci's brother, and Isabella's lawyer.

"Care to dance?" His hand was already on the small of her back as she nodded and moved towards him. She'd known Travis forever and he was a great guy; many would even consider him a catch. Travis was tall, just over six foot two and had hair as dark as hers. His eyes were dark, too—a deep brown that suited his intense moodiness well.

Isabella glanced toward the table where they'd been sitting and saw that Aidan wasn't there. Her eyes searched the dance floor and then found him, dancing with Missy. She frowned and Travis caught her. He'd seen it all.

"So, that's who you've set your sights on next?" His tone was teasing and she wanted to smack him. It was a little embarrassing to be caught like that. Especially if it turned out that Aidan wasn't interested or, worse yet, that he was interested in Missy.

"I haven't set my sights on anyone," she said. "I wouldn't mind, though. I'll admit that. Why? You don't think we'd make a good couple?" She could tease right back.

Travis snapped, "I don't think he's right for you."

His forceful tone surprised her.

"No? Why not? He's a successful artist, and a good person. We grew up with Aidan."

"He's a nice enough guy. Just seems a little dull. I see you with someone a bit more exciting."

"Yeah? I don't know about that." Isabella was intrigued with Aidan and didn't think he seemed remotely boring.

"I just don't see it," Travis said again.

"Okay, who do you think would be right for me then?" she asked. As much as Travis's bossiness could be annoying, she did respect his opinion.

He was silent for a moment and then muttered, "I have no idea." When the music ended, he pulled away from her and said, "I'm going to get a drink. Do you need anything?"

"No, I'm good. I think I'm going to have another piece of cake." Travis smiled at that as he turned toward the bar and Isabella made her way back to the table, where Uncle Jim had several pieces of cake lined up in front of him.

"I saved one for you. Had a feeling you'd be back for more," he said with a wink as she sat down.

"You know me so well. Thank you." Isabella loved wedding cake and this one was especially delicious. It was a super-moist lemon sponge cake with raspberry jam filling and lemon buttercream frosting. She was on her last bite when Jen swooped in and sat in the empty seat next to her.

"My feet are killing me," she said as she reached for one of Uncle Jim's extra slices.

"The shoes are gorgeous, though," Isabella said.

"Absolutely, worth every bit of torture they're putting me through," Jen agreed as she shoved a big bite of cake in her mouth.

Isabella glanced around, wondering if Aidan and Aunt Edna were still there.

"They're gone, left just a few minutes ago. They came by the head table first, to say goodbye."

"It's so early." Isabella tried to hide her disappointment.

"Aunt Edna hasn't been feeling great lately, I heard. She did well to come at all."

"Oh, I didn't realize that."

"It's nothing serious. Aidan said she was feeling a bit under the weather."

"She's a delightful woman, that Edna," Uncle Jim interjected and Isabella smiled in agreement.

"Besides, what do you care? You've got Travis here to dance with," Jen teased.

"It's not like that with Travis. You know that. He's my friend, and my lawyer."

"He's hot. I don't know why you don't go out with him. I swear he seems interested."

"Even if he is, I'm not. And even if I was, I don't think it's smart to mix business and personal."

"Hmmm." Jen looked thoughtful for a moment. "It might not be smart, but I bet it sure would be fun."

TRAVIS JONES NURSED HIS JACK AND COKE AND, NOT FOR THE first time, wished he had a crush on someone else, anyone but Isabella Graham. As long as he could remember, it had been Isabella, and no one except his sister Traci knew. Traci knew everything, though. It was part of being a twin. He'd never said a word about Isabella to anyone, but he didn't need to with Traci. They were both in tune with what the other was feeling, and she'd sensed it almost immediately. All it had taken was a glance, one look that Traci happened to catch, and she'd understood. But that didn't mean she liked it. Especially when Isabella started dating his best friend, Christian. He'd hated that. But he couldn't blame Christian. He'd never said a word to him about how he felt, until they broke up, and then he jokingly asked Christian if he'd mind if he asked her out. He made light of it, as if it was no big deal, and Christian was fine with it. What did he care? He was madly in love with Molly.

He took another sip of his drink and from a distance watched Isabella dance again, with her Uncle Jim. She looked beautiful as her uncle twirled her around and led her expertly across the dance floor.

"I saw you dance with her earlier. Have you asked her out yet?" Traci sat in the chair next to him. He'd never seen his sister look so beautiful. She was glowing, and sweating a little from dancing to the last five songs. Her new husband, Dan, was heading their way with a round of drinks. Travis approved of Dan. He was Christian's brother and a good guy. He loved Traci and made her happy and that was all that mattered. He and Traci had always been super close, and she was staring at him, waiting for a response.

"No, not yet."

"What are you waiting for? I have to admit, you did look good together."

"You sound surprised," Travis chuckled.

"Well, I'm not sure if Isabella would be my first choice for you."

"You don't like her," he said flatly.

"No, I do. Of course I do. She's Jen's sister, after all, and she's beautiful. She just—well, she just seems like a handful. Are you sure you want the drama?"

"Isabella is a good kid."

"Right. So, go ask her out already." Traci gave him a little shove and laughed as Dan handed her a glass of wine. She leaned over and whispered, "Here's your opportunity. She's coming this way."

Travis glanced up. Isabella and her Uncle Jim were walking toward them.

"Traci, we are heading out now. Everything was wonderful, thank you." Isabella gave both Dan and Traci hugs good-bye and wished them well on their honeymoon. They were flying out the next day for a week in the Caribbean, Turks and Caicos. "Travis, take care. I'm sure I'll see you soon." She moved in to give him a hug good-bye and he pulled her in tight, for just a second, and then shook her Uncle Jim's hand and wished them both a good night.

"Chicken," Traci said with a laugh as they walked away.

"Timing wasn't right," Travis said. He knew he'd be seeing Isabella in the coming week. He handled most of her real estate closings and she had a few deals pending.

"Well, better make your move fast. Jen says she has an interest in Aidan," Traci teased.

"So, I've heard."

CHAPTER 2

Isabella was a morning person. It was her favorite time of day. She sipped from a cup of rich, dark roast coffee and gazed out the window at the sun coming up over the mountains. Her condo overlooked a small pond and she loved watching the surface water ripple in the breeze. It was so peaceful, and she'd instantly felt at home the moment she'd walked in the door four years ago.

"Mew." The fluffy cat got her attention as she rubbed against Isabella's leg and demanded to be fed.

"What's the matter, Jolene? You didn't like the food?" Isabella scooped up the small cat that was all fur and gave her a hug. She walked over to her dish, which was untouched. Jolene had rejected the morning's offering.

"Really? You don't like that one, either?" Jolene responded by purring and rubbing against her neck.

"Fine, I'll open something else for you. You're spoiled rotten, you know." She set her down and rummaged around for another can of food that might be more acceptable and switched the bowls. Jolene indicated her approval and dug in.

Isabella topped off her coffee and sat back down. She loved

that little cat. She'd rescued Jolene eight years ago from a local shelter, and she'd been about five then. The shelter volunteers said her family had moved away and just left her behind. Stories like that broke her heart. Isabella had never had a long-haired cat before and had assumed she'd get a short-haired one, like her family had always had. But, when she walked into the shelter, the beautiful and unusually tiny Maine Coon cat had walked right over to her, rubbed against her legs and that was it. Her name, Jolene, suited her perfectly.

Isabella thought about the day ahead, going over everything that was pending and needed her attention. She was busy; there was a lot of activity going on and that was a good thing. She thrived on being busy. She loved the real estate business and was good at it. Her original plan, after graduating from the University of Montana with a degree in business administration, had been to move to Bozeman or even Billings, though she'd liked the idea of Bozeman better as it was closer to home. She figured there'd be more opportunities for recent graduates in either city. But then she'd seen an ad for a real estate firm that had just opened on Main Street in Beauville. They were hiring new agents with no experience, and it was mid-May. If she got the job, she could give it the summer to see how it went, and if it didn't work out, she could look for something else in the fall.

It had worked out better than she'd ever imagined. Isabella had taken to selling real estate right away. She loved the independence and entrepreneurial nature of it and she was a naturally competitive hard worker. She also had an intuitive feel for the business and was a great match-maker of people and houses. Although she was a veteran of the field now, with almost twelve years of experience, she still got just as excited as she had her first year whenever she got a new listing or made a sale. She glanced at the clock and quickly finished the rest of her coffee. She didn't want to be late for the Monday morning meeting.

ISABELLA GRABBED A JELLY DOUGHNUT AND POURED HERSELF another cup of coffee when she arrived in the office, then settled into the conference room with a few minutes to spare after saying a quick hello to her best friend, Anna, who was also the office manager. At nine o'clock on the dot, Dottie MacDonald, the firm president, entered the room and sat at the head of the table. Dottie had been in the business forever. She was around sixty and was a dynamo. She was short and a bit on the plump side, but she hid it well as she loved fashion and was always dressed beautifully. Her hair was a perfect, blonde bob that fell just past her chin and Isabella didn't think she'd ever seen her without her signature strand of pearls.

Dottie called the meeting to order and they began as they always did, by going around the room and discussing what they had for pending activity, any new listings coming up and any that were due to expire. They were a team of eight, which could seem like a lot for a small town like Beauville, but they also served the surrounding towns, including Bozeman, which was just a half-hour away. Plus, not all of their agents were full-time. Half of them were semi-retired and just worked part-time to keep busy, for something to do. Real estate tended to have somewhat high turnover, due to the one hundred percent commission sales factor, and Dottie was always on the lookout for new agents. She liked to have them start in pairs, as it was likely that one, or sometimes even both, might not make it. At nine thirty, just as they were winding down, there was a knock on the door, and Dottie got up to open it.

"Great. Come on in, you two, and take a seat." Dottie

turned to the rest of the team. "Everyone, this is Melissa Atwell and Jake Evans. Please welcome them and make them feel at home." Isabella watched as Missy and Jake found empty seats at the end of the table. She knew that Missy was about her age, thirty-three, and Jake looked to be in his mid-twenties.

"Some of you may know Missy from the elementary school, where she was a teacher for a number of years. Jake just recently graduated from the University of Montana and is excited to put his business degree to good use." Dottie looked around the table and her gaze hovered over Isabella and Bill Williams, another senior agent. Bill and Isabella were the two top agents and Bill was a great guy. He was about ten years older than Isabella and was a family man with two small children and a lovely, stay-at-home wife. Everyone loved Bill, including Isabella. He was impossible not to like.

"So, I was thinking, Bill, why don't you take Jake, and Isabella, you take Missy? They can shadow with you both for the next few weeks and you can show them the ropes."

Isabella smiled at Missy and mentally cursed Dottie. She hated training new people and Dottie knew it. But, as Dottie had also explained to Isabella, if she did it well, it would be worth her while. She'd get a percentage of any deals that Missy closed for her first year, so theoretically it benefited her to mentor and guide her. Isabella knew it would slow her down, though, and she wasn't the most patient person to begin with. But, she thought of her Uncle Jim, and also knew this was something she needed to work on.

MONDAYS WERE ALWAYS BUSY, AND THIS ONE WAS EVEN MORE hectic now that Isabella had Missy shadowing her. It would be a good first day for her, though, as she could see a bit of everything. Isabella had several showings scheduled throughout the day, as well as a presentation for a new listing and a counter-offer that had been accepted. When they broke for lunch, Isabella took Melissa to Delancey's, which was the nicest restaurant in town. Normally, she just grabbed a salad and ate at her desk, but Dottie always liked them to take new people out to lunch on their first day, to make them feel special and to give them a "taste of success" as she put it.

They both ordered salads with grilled chicken and chatted easily while they were waiting for their food to arrive. The morning had been non-stop as they raced from one meeting to the next, and then handled all the paperwork for the offer. This was the first chance they had to really talk, and Isabella was curious to find out why Melissa had decided to go into real estate.

"Honestly, I burned out on teaching and I couldn't really see myself just in an office, behind a desk all day. I've always been interested in real estate. I like fixing up houses and I love the idea of being around adults all day instead of seven- and eight-year-olds."

Isabella shuddered at the thought of it. She admired those who could teach and knew she wouldn't last a week in the job.

"How's your family?" Isabella asked as she reached for the roll she'd told herself she wasn't going to have.

"They're great. Mom's a volunteer at the library. She loves that, and Dad is still teaching in Bozeman at the University. Ryan's doing awesome, too. His painting business has taken off and he just hired two new guys to help him handle all the work that has been coming in. Christian has referred him quite a bit of business." Missy looked as though she wished could take back what she'd just said about Christian, and Isabella set her at ease.

"It's okay. There are no hard feelings with Christian. We're friends now."

"Oh, I'm so glad to hear that. I've seen them a few times lately and his wife Molly seems so nice."

"Yes, she is. They're well-suited." Their salads arrived and they both dug in. Isabella didn't realize that Melissa's brother's business was doing so well. She'd have to keep that in mind as she was often asked for referrals. New homeowners almost always had a few changes they wanted to make once they moved in.

"So, have you thought about your prospect list?" she asked Melissa. One of the first things that Dottie had new agents do was to draw up a list of everyone they knew and to prioritize the ones that might be thinking of buying or selling real estate in the near future.

"Yes, I've been working on that. My first client may actually stop in later this afternoon. He said he'd call first, of course, to make sure we'll be there."

"Oh? That's great. Who is it?"

"Aidan."

Isabella set her fork down in surprise.

"Really? I didn't realize you knew him that well."

Melissa smiled. "We go way back. Aidan is a good friend and we've kept in touch over the years. He seems excited to settle here."

This was an interesting development, and could be the opportunity she'd been looking for to spend more time with Aidan. Of course, he was Melissa's client, and she was training her, so they'd be inseparable for the next few weeks. It might be difficult to get time alone with him, but she'd have to figure out a way.

A FEW MINUTES BEFORE THEY ARRIVED BACK AT THE OFFICE, Missy got a call from Aidan, saying he was on his way and could be there in ten minutes if that worked for them. Missy confirmed, and when they sat down at Isabella's desk to start a search on the computer for Aidan, Missy pulled some papers out of a folder and handed them to her.

"I ran this search at home, using the loose parameters Aidan mentioned already, the area of the town he prefers, ideal size, number of bedrooms, things like that"

Isabella took the papers and glanced through them.

"When did you do this?"

"Last night, just in case Aidan was able to come in today. I know it's not from the office computers, so I may have missed some listings, but hopefully it will give you an idea."

Isabella was impressed. Missy had come up with a good list.

"It's pretty close. There might be one or two newer listings that aren't on here, but overall, this looks great."

Missy smiled and Isabella showed her how to run a search on their in-house system. It connected to the national MLS listings, so the office could access all area listings as soon as they went live. As she predicted, the list Isabella's search generated was identical to Missy's with the addition of two new listings that had been added that day.

When Aidan arrived, Anna brought him into a small conference room that they used to meet with new clients and a moment later, they went in to join him.

"Hi, Aidan, nice to see you again," Isabella said as he rose from his chair to greet them.

"Thanks for seeing me on such short notice." They all sat back down and Isabella pulled out a small notepad.

"Missy filled me in on what you are looking for, but I'd love to learn a little more. What would your dream house be like, if you could make a wish list? What's most important?" Isabella loved to ask these questions, to help the client dream a bit but then to also ferret out what the 'must-haves' were. It often fascinated her how the houses her clients fell in love with were often quite different from what they initially said they were looking for.

Missy had her notebook out, too, and as soon as Aidan started talking, she began furiously scribbling notes.

"Privacy, and a lot of light," Aidan began, and was then silent for a moment, considering the question. "Open spaces, high ceilings—cathedral ceilings, actually, would be great. Big windows, lots of glass. I guess a more contemporary style, but I'm not looking for anything too fancy. I need a big room to work in. A loft would be ideal, and a few extra bedrooms. Plenty of room to spread out, but not too big. After all, it's just me." He smiled at that and Isabella nodded. While he was talking, she'd been mentally assessing the different houses on the list they'd come up with earlier. None of them were a good match based on what he was saying was important to him.

"What is your budget?" Isabella asked. The list that Missy had generated was a fairly low price-point, typical first-time buyer range. If Aidan was able to be more flexible, that might open up some possibilities. There were several houses that came to mind right away, but they were in a much higher price range and on larger lots of land. But, he'd said privacy was important.

Aidan mentioned a range that was triple the amount Missy had been working with. All of the houses she'd been thinking of could work now.

"I have a few places in mind that could be good possibilities for you. If you don't mind waiting for a moment, I'm going to steal Missy and then we'll be back with a few listing sheets for you to look over."

When they got back to her desk, Isabella ran a new search and printed out the three houses that had come to mind. All were gorgeous and modern, and on several acres of land.

"I had no idea he'd be looking in that range. I'm sorry." Missy said as Isabella handed her the printouts of the listings.

"Nothing to be sorry about. We all do it, make assumptions about what the range will be, and are often surprised. Sometimes pleasantly."

When they settled back in the conference room, Isabella went over the listings with him and he seemed excited.

"These all look great. When can we see them?"

"I should be able to arrange showings for tomorrow, if that works?"

"Perfect."

"Great. Missy will give you a call to confirm once we've set it up."

"I appreciate it. I'll see you both tomorrow."

CHAPTER 3

After work, Isabella headed to her mother's house. She had called earlier in the day and left a message with Anna to tell Isabella to plan on dinner with the family that evening. They often got together on Monday evenings and Isabella welcomed the invite. The last thing she felt like doing after a long, busy Monday was cooking.

Jen and Uncle Jim were already in the kitchen when she arrived. Jen was chopping tomatoes to add to a large bowl of tossed salad, while Uncle Jim sat on one of the island stools, drinking a glass of milk, and observing it all.

"What can I do?" Isabella asked her mother.

"There's a loaf of fresh Italian bread on the counter. Do you want to cut that up?" Isabella found the bread and started slicing.

Meanwhile, her mother stirred a pot of red sauce that was simmering on the stove. She adjusted the heat on the burner next to it, where a large pot of pasta was cooking. Using a fork, she fished out a piece of ziti, dipped the end in the sauce and then handed it to her husband, Tom, to take a bite. They'd been married for ten years now, and Isabella was pleased to see her mother so happy, finally. Tom was a good man, and adored her mother.

"What do you think? Is it done?" she asked him.

"It's perfect," Tom said. "Let's eat."

Her mother brought the pasta and meatballs to the table and they all sat down and dug in.

"How's the book coming?" Isabella asked her sister as she reached for a slice of bread. Jen was a best-selling romance author who often traveled to research the exotic settings that she used in her books. Her last trip had been a long one. She'd gone to Ireland and Scotland and had planned to spend a week in each and then come home. But, her stay in Ireland had been extended to nearly two months after she met an intriguing Irishman in a local bar. They'd actually all met Ian recently, when he surprised Jen by showing up at a party she'd jokingly invited him to. Isabella had been impressed, and had a feeling she knew where her sister's next 'research' trip might take her.

"It's good. I'm a little stuck on where to go next, but I'll figure it out."

"You always do," Uncle Jim said with a smile, then asked Isabella, "How was your day?"

"Good, but busy. Missy started today," Isabella told them. "She's training with me."

Jen made a face. "Lucky you." She knew how much Isabella hated training new people.

"She might be okay, actually. She already has her first client."

"No kidding? That's fast," Jen said, as she shook more parmesan cheese over her pasta.

"Interesting one, too. It's Aidan; turns out they're good friends."

Jen looked up. "That is interesting. Nice way for you to

spend some time with him." After a minute she added, "unless there's something between them? Did they ever date?"

"Not that I know of," Isabella said, and then added, "I got the impression they were just friends."

"Well, that's a good thing, and great that he wants to buy something. Sounds like he might stick around for a while."

"That's what he said. We have a few places lined up to show him tomorrow."

They finished eating, and after they helped their mother clear the table, she set down a freshly baked cheesecake and a side of raspberry sauce. Isabella and Jen hesitated for a moment then both reached for a slice. It was impossible to pass up their mother's cheesecake.

"What are you up to this weekend?" Jen asked with a mischievous gleam in her eye as she prepared to take a bite.

"No plans yet. What did you have in mind?"

"Well, you know I joined that local kayak club?" Isabella didn't know that. It was hard to keep up with Jen's many interests. She was always trying something new.

"No, is that a new thing?"

"Yes, and no. I actually joined it last year when I was dating Jason and he bought me a kayak for my birthday. I joined the club right after, but a few weeks later, we broke up. He insisted I keep the kayak."

"So, you've been using it?" No one had ever given Isabella a kayak. She smiled at the idea of it. It wasn't likely that anyone ever would. Jewelry, yes. Kayak, not so much.

"Well, since Ian went home, I've had a little too much time on my hands and went to a meeting last weekend, and had a blast. There's a big group of us going out on the river this weekend, and I thought you might want to come with us. It's a relatively calm river. Good for beginners, they say."

"Do you know me?" Isabella laughed at her sister. "When have you ever seen me near a kayak?"

"Oh, come on, it'll be fun. You might love it."

"I don't think I'm ready to step that far out of my comfort zone. You can tell me all about it when you get back." The thought of it, of getting wet and lugging around a heavy kayak, just didn't appeal to her in the slightest. Maybe she'd treat herself to a mani-pedi instead. A new place had recently opened up and they did a wonderful job. Much nicer to relax with a soothing, warm paraffin soak and a sweet-smelling sugar citrus scrub, followed by a muscle-melting calf and foot massage. Yes, that was much more up her alley.

"What are you going to do instead? Get a pedicure or something?" Jen teased her sister and then laughed when Isabella's expression must have given it away. "You are! I knew it. That sounds fun, too," she said wistfully.

"Come with me," Isabella said. "It will be way better than kayaking."

"No, I'm excited for this trip. I'll do a pedicure with you another time, though. I've been dying to check out that new place."

"Besides, even if I wanted to, I can't. I have food pantry duty in the morning." Isabella was a volunteer at the local food pantry and usually worked one or two shifts a month, in addition to helping with the ordering of the food and general administration.

"Oh, that's right. I'm sure someone could fill in for you, though, if you wanted to come. Mom probably would, right?"

"Jen, I have no interest in kayaking!" Isabella laughed, and helped herself to another meatball as her sister sighed and finally gave up.

"Fine, but one of these days, I want to get you to come with me. Kayaking is a blast, and it's a great stress reliever."

"I'm not stressed," Isabella said.

"Everyone is stressed to some degree, honey," her mother added as she reached for the salad.

"I have one you can borrow," Uncle Jim said.

"You have a kayak?" Uncle Jim never failed to amaze her.

"Picked it up a few years ago. Still take it out every now and again, but just down to my little pond. That's more my speed. You kids can have the river." He paused for a moment, looking at Isabella thoughtfully before adding, "You know, men like to kayak. You should go. Never know who you might meet."

Isabella chuckled at that; Uncle Jim loved to play match-maker. "Okay, Jen can scope it out for me. If there are some hot guys, maybe I will go sometime," she said with a chuckle, but she didn't really mean it. Cute guys or not, the odds of that happening were slim.

———

ISABELLA GOT TO WORK A LITTLE EARLIER THAN USUAL THE next day and Anna was already there and had the coffee brewing. She poured them each a cup and motioned for Isabella to join her in the conference room. Anna was the same age as Isabella and they'd started there years ago, just a week apart, and quickly became best friends. Anna had no interest in the sales side of the business, though. She was great with numbers, and handled all the bookkeeping for the office as well as the marketing and anything else that needed doing.

Anna had married Rob, her college sweetheart, right after they graduated, and for years everyone thought they were the perfect couple, and then the perfect family when they had two children, Emily and Bobby, born a year apart. Irish twins, Anna sometimes joked, as the two were often inseparable. Her perfect marriage had come to an abrupt halt, though, when Anna discovered a disposable cell phone in Rob's gym bag. Assuming it was there by mistake and belonged to someone at the gym, she started scrolling through the text messages to see who owned it. A shocking, naked image that was sent from the phone confirmed that the owner was Rob, and he was up to no good. He was messaging with several women, sending suggestive texts and inappropriate pictures.

He tried, lamely, to explain, and then to beg and plead for Anna to forgive him. He insisted that it didn't mean anything, that Anna was the only one he'd ever love. But, Anna wasn't having any of it. She called Travis the next day, and he did a great job handling the divorce. That was over a year ago. Rob had moved out immediately, and Anna moved on. Sort of. She seemed to be doing well enough after making it through a tough first year alone. But, she still showed no interest in dating, although she loved to hear every detail of Isabella's dating dramas.

"So, fill me in. We didn't get a minute to talk yesterday, with Missy glued to your side. I saw Aidan come in, and you're helping him find a house? How perfect."

"He's actually Missy's client. They're pretty tight, I guess. But, the good news is that since Missy has to shadow me for a few weeks, I'll be spending time with him, too."

"You know, I think I heard rumors years ago that they dated," Anna said thoughtfully. "But, that was a long time ago. She was just recently dating Jeremy Smith, I think, wasn't she?"

"Maybe, I'm not really sure. She hasn't mentioned that she's dating anyone." The front door opened. Missy walked in and Anna and Isabella started to make their way back to their desks.

"Don't forget, we're on for dinner at Jen's Saturday night,"

Isabella reminded Anna as she stopped by the kitchen and topped off her coffee.

"I'm looking forward to it," Anna said. "Rob is taking the kids that night so it works out perfectly."

Aidan met Isabella and Missy at the office early that afternoon and they set off to look at the three houses Isabella had found for him.

The first was the biggest of the three homes, probably more house than he needed, but it was in his range, and Isabella remembered being impressed with it when they'd gone on the MLS tour a few weeks back. Whenever a new house came on the market, they usually had an open house just for agents to tour and get familiar with the property before showing it to their clients. This one had a feature that she thought Aidan might appreciate.

They parked and then Isabella let them into the house. Right away, Missy immediately started to ooh and ah. The house really was lovely, with enormous floor-to-ceiling windows, gleaming hardwood floors, exposed beams and a large kitchen with modern, stainless steel appliances and sleek, black granite countertops.

Aidan was silent as they walked around the home until they reached the upstairs loft, which ran the entire length of the family room below and was glowing with all the sunlight that poured in.

"This is incredible." He gazed out the window and then back around the room, assessing it.

"Could you paint here?" Missy asked.

"Yes. The light is amazing. It would make a great studio."

"What's your studio like in New York?" Isabella asked, curious about what his life had been like there.

"Everything is much smaller there. It was about half the size of this room, and much darker, though the morning light wasn't too bad. That's when I did my best work."

"Do you still need to go back and pack up?" Missy asked. They'd asked Aidan if he needed to sell his place there before buying something else, but he'd assured them that he was just renting there.

"No. I rented the place furnished, so didn't have much there, mostly clothes and painting supplies. Everything is here now, so I don't have to go back for anything."

They made their way through the rest of the house, through the four bedrooms, finished basement and multi-car garage. Isabella noticed with amusement that Aidan seemed distracted, and guessed that he was mentally back in the loft, picturing himself setting up his painting materials and settling in.

They still had two other houses to visit. Both were perfectly nice homes, impressive even, but Isabella didn't even have to ask if Aidan had a favorite; it was obvious. The first house was the clear winner. The most important thing to him was a place to paint, with good light and the other two homes, as lovely as they were, didn't even come close in comparison. She had suspected he'd fall in love with that loft.

When they got back to the office, Isabella led Missy and Aidan into the conference room.

"Coffee, anyone? I know I'm ready for a cup." It was nearly three and Isabella usually had a cup every afternoon. Still a bit distracted, Aidan just nodded, while Missy jumped up to get the coffee for them. Isabella motioned for her to sit down.

"Thanks, Missy. I'll get it for us. Be right back." She returned with three coffees and joined them at the round table.

"So, Aidan, what do you think? We can try and set up a few more showings later in the week if you like."

"Is there anything else like the first house?"

Isabella knew what he was asking. "You mean with a room like that loft?"

Aidan nodded.

"No, there's nothing else that has a room like that. There're a few other houses we could look at that are in the same range, but no rooms that have that kind of space and light."

"Good, because I can't imagine I'd find something I'd like more than that one. It's perfect."

"Are you sure?" Missy asked.

He looked at her fondly. "Yeah, I'm sure. I don't need to see anything else to know which one is right for me. I knew the minute I saw that one."

Isabella smiled. It was rare that it was this easy, but wonderful when it was.

"Did you want to put an offer in?" she asked.

Aidan hesitated for a long moment, as his fingers rhythmically tapped on the table. He wasn't looking at either of them, just seemed lost in his thoughts. Finally, he broke the silence and said, "Yes, let's do this."

They talked numbers for a few minutes, then Isabella drew up the paperwork for an offer and called the listing agent to present his offer verbally, following up with the signed offer letter by fax. The listing agent had twenty-four hours to get back to them with a response, and as it was already late afternoon. She didn't expect that they'd hear back until the next day. Aidan had made a strong offer, just a bit below the asking price, so Isabella was confident that they'd be able to work something out.

About twenty minutes later, as they were walking him out, Isabella's cell phone rang and it was the listing agent. When she finished the call, she turned to the others who'd already gathered from overhearing her part of the conversation that the news was good.

"Congratulations! The owner has accepted your offer. They're not even counter-offering because you came so close to the asking price."

"Aidan, that's wonderful!" Missy exclaimed and gave him a hug, while he stood there, looking dazed and happy.

"I just bought a house," he said in wonder. "Thank you, both of you."

He left, and as Isabella and Missy walked back to their desks, Isabella said, "It's almost never that easy. Just so you know, this wasn't at all typical. Usually, it can drag on for weeks or months, or even longer as people want to keep seeing houses until they find the perfect one."

"Well, it may be beginner's luck, but it works for me," Missy said. "I'm really thrilled for Aidan. That house seems meant to be for him."

"It does seem meant to be," Isabella agreed.

CHAPTER 4

Travis glancedout his office window again. Isabella and Missy were on their way over to pick up copies of the purchase and sale agreement for Aidan to sign. Isabella had called yesterday after Aidan's offer was accepted and asked him to start on the paperwork for the P & S, which would be the next step in the process, once the home inspection was done. After that, the mortgage processing, checking the deed, and so on, would follow and if all went well, Aidan would sign the closing papers in about a month or so.

Outside his office door, Travis heard Mrs. Crosby humming softly along with the radio and smiled to himself. Christian had suggested when he first opened the office years ago that he should get himself a hot secretary. He wasn't opposed to the idea, but when Mrs. Crosby, a plump, fifty-something grandmother, walked in to the interview, he'd hired her on the spot. She was amazing, and had been a legal secretary for years before coming to work for him. She was great with clients, and made sure things ran smoothly. She also mothered him a bit, but he didn't mind. Mrs. Crosby was a better cook than his own mother, and who would complain about the occasional fresh baked muffin with their morning coffee?

As a small-town lawyer, Travis was a generalist, handling a bit of everything, though the bulk of his practice was a combination of real estate and wills and estates, with the occasional divorce or petty crime thrown in to keep things interesting. He liked the variety, and his practice had grown over the years so that he had a good reputation and made a comfortable living. He could probably have made partner by now at some bigger law firm in Bozeman, but that thought had never appealed to him. He liked working in a small town, where he knew just about everyone, and if he wanted to duck out early on a Friday to go fishing or play a little golf, he could. It wasn't often that he did, but on those days, he always sent Mrs. Crosby home early, too. He felt she deserved the break as much as he did.

He turned his chair at the sound of Isabella's laugh, as Mrs. Crosby showed her and Missy into his office. They were chuckling about shopping or something. He hadn't caught the conversation, but they all seemed to be in a good mood.

Isabella and Missy sat in the two chairs opposite his desk. He picked up a file folder and flipped through the pages before handing them to Missy.

"Here you go. I understand this is your first sale and that congratulations are in order."

Missy beamed. "Thank you. I'm excited." She glanced Isabella's way and added, "Though I know it won't always go this easily."

Isabella's phone dinged, signaling a text message, and she glanced down, then frowned.

"Something wrong?" Travis asked.

"Oh, it's nothing. Just annoying. The other girl who is supposed to work the food pantry with me Saturday morning is canceling and I have no idea who I can get to fill in."

"I'd do it if I was here, but we're heading to Billings for the weekend," Missy said.

"I'll do it," Travis said.

Isabella hesitated. "You've never volunteered there before. Are you sure?"

"How hard can it be? We just hand out food, right? You can show me what to do."

Isabella smiled and looked relieved. "If you're sure, that would be great. We're short-handed right now for volunteers. I could ask Molly's mom or Aunt Betty, but they've already picked up some extra shifts this month."

"Then it's all set. Just tell me what time to be there."

"He seems nice," Missy said as they left Travis's office and climbed into Isabella's navy blue Audi sedan.

"Travis? He's great. We've been friends forever."

"Just friends? I thought I picked up a vibe, maybe."

Isabella shot Missy a look of surprise. "from Travis? I don't think so. Maybe he's interested in you?"

Missy laughed at that. "No. I can tell when a guy I've just met is interested. It wasn't like that. What's his deal? Seems like a good catch for someone."

"He's a great guy. I don't really think he's the settling down type, though. I rarely see him with the same girl for longer than a month or two. Everyone thought he was going to marry Ellen Shores a few years back. They'd been together for five years or so, but they broke up and he hasn't been serious with anyone since. Not that I know of, anyway."

Before Missy could change the subject, Isabella couldn't stop herself from asking. "What about you and Aidan? Did you two used to date? You seem really comfortable with each other."

Missy hesitated for a moment before answering. "Yeah, we dated years ago, before Aidan moved to New York. He wanted me to move with him, but my family and my life is here. Mom wasn't doing well for a while, so it was never really an option. Aidan understood. We kind of drifted apart after that. It's been nice re-connecting again."

Isabella found herself involuntarily frowning at that.

"Are you getting back together?" she wondered out loud.

"Me and Aidan?" Missy sounded surprised. "No. It's been great seeing him again, but that was a long time ago. We've both moved on. Besides, I've been dating Jeremy Miles for a few months now."

"Jeremy Miles? I had no idea." Jeremy was a mortician. He grew up in the business as his family owned the local funeral home. He was a really nice guy; everyone loved Jeremy.

Isabella pulled in to her usual spot in front of the office. She debated whether or not to ask about Aidan's status, though it sounded like Missy was no longer interested, so why not?

"So, is Aidan dating anyone?" she asked casually as they got out of the car.

"I don't think so. He hasn't been back here very long." They were just about at the front door when the light finally dawned for Missy.

"Are you interested in Aidan?"

"I don't know." Isabella felt flustered for some reason. "It's been so long since I've spent any time with him. I wouldn't mind getting to know him better."

Missy was quiet for a moment, then said, "I have an idea. I'm supposed to go to some art show in Bozeman with him this Sunday night, but Jeremy's parents want to have us over for dinner and it would just be a little weird for him to have to explain to his parents that his girlfriend is out with another guy, even though we're just friends. Maybe you can go instead?"

This was too good to be true.

"I'd love to go. If he'd be okay with that." She hoped he would be; it would be the perfect chance to get to know him better.

"I'll talk to him tomorrow. I'm sure he won't mind. I'll just say we were talking and I mentioned that I have to cancel and you said it sounded fun so I suggested you go. Sound good?"

"Sounds perfect," Isabella agreed.

ISABELLA ARRIVED AT THE FOOD PANTRY A HALF-HOUR EARLY ON Saturday. She liked to get there ahead of time to check inventory and see how much meat and staples like eggs, milk and cheese they had on hand as those were the most in-demand items. She'd told Travis to get there at about a quarter to ten. The pantry officially opened at ten, but there was always a line when they first opened. As one of several coordinators of the pantry, Isabella handled the monthly reports, adding up how many people used the pantry each month.

It didn't take long to do, about ten minutes or so, and Isabella was in a great mood as she sipped the coffee that she'd brought with her. She'd been in a good mood all week, actually, since Missy confirmed that she'd talked to Aidan and it was fine by him if Isabella went in her place to the art opening. He'd called the office Friday afternoon to touch base with her and said he'd be by Sunday afternoon around four to pick her up and head into Bozeman.

Isabella turned when there was a light tap on the door and then Travis walked in. There were already a few people waiting outside.

"Morning," she called out as Travis shut the door behind him.

"How's it going?" Travis glanced at the pages of numbers in front of her.

"Good. I just finished totaling up the numbers for the main food bank that gives us most of our food."

Isabella showed him around the pantry, pointing out where everything was and explained that they would each take a client around the pantry and help them shop, picking out the items that they wanted, and the size of their family would determine how many they received.

"How long have you been volunteering here?" Travis asked.

Isabella had to stop and think about that. "About eight years, maybe? It's been a while."

"No kidding? How did you get involved?"

"I'd been thinking about doing some kind of volunteering and the timing seemed right when Patty, who started the pantry and ran it for over twenty years, announced her retirement. It was a big job for one person, so the church decided to make it more manageable by having three people split up the duties. There's also a team of volunteers that work the shifts once or twice a month."

"And you enjoy it?"

"It's important to me. We were once clients of this pantry." It was long ago, but Isabella still remembered the stress of those days. "Money was really tight for a while after my dad died. He didn't have much in the way of insurance and left my mother with a pile of bills. It took her a long time to climb out of that debt. She was embarrassed to come here, but she did, for a few months to keep food on the table until things got better."

"That must have been tough," Travis sympathized.

"It was. I don't ever want to be in that position again, and I know how hard it is for most of these people to come here, especially when it's their first time."

Travis glanced out the window. "There's a lot of people out there now. Is it always this busy?"

Isabella glanced at the clock. It was a few minutes before ten, but she didn't mind opening early since they were ready to go.

"We always have a mad rush when we first open. People like to come early, before we start to run out of things."

"Do you think we'll have enough?"

"We should be okay. We are low on cheese, but have plenty of eggs, meat and milk."

Isabella opened the door and invited the first two clients in. They worked steadily for the next hour-and-a-half, until the line outside finally died down. For the last half-hour they had an occasional straggler, just enough to keep them busy until closing time came at noon.

"Thanks so much for filling in," Isabella said as they got ready to lock up.

"It was fun. I was happy to help out." Travis had done a great job. He was patient with the clients and made them feel at ease.

"What are you up to the rest of the weekend?" Travis asked as they walked out to their cars.

"Jen is having Anna and me over for dinner tonight. Jen's kayaking today, and tried to talk me into going with her. Can you imagine?" She laughed at the thought. "Oh, and tomorrow afternoon I'm going to some art show thing with Aidan."

"You have a date with Aidan?" Travis frowned at that.

"No, not a date. Not really. Missy was supposed to go, but had something else come up and asked if I wanted to go instead."

"And you jumped at the chance," he said flatly.

"Well, yeah. What's wrong, you don't like Aidan?"

Travis was quiet for a minute. "He's fine. I just don't see him with you, that's all."

"No? Why not?" Isabella was curious as Travis had said something similar at the wedding, too.

"No reason, really. I just don't see it. I could be wrong, though. I often am," he said with a wry smile.

"So, what are you up to? Do you have a hot date?" she teased him.

"A hot date? I was hoping to, but she's busy tonight, with her girlfriends," he teased back.

"Very funny. You're always with someone different. I can't keep up."

"I'm not that bad," he protested.

"I've never seen you serious about anyone—well, except for Ellen. But that was ages ago. Whatever happened there? Everyone thought you two would get engaged."

Travis looked like he was trying to come up with an explanation and Isabella immediately regretted asking the question.

"Never mind, I shouldn't have asked. That's too personal."

"No, it's okay. It's just kind of awkward and not something I'm proud of. We were together for so long that getting engaged was the next step and I just couldn't do it. I should have ended things sooner than I did, but it was comfortable and breaking up is hard. It sounds like the world's biggest cliche but although I loved her, I wasn't in love with her. I couldn't take that next step."

"Well, you did the right thing, then." Isabella thought of all the people she knew who probably never should have gotten married.

"Well, have fun at your girls' dinner tonight," Travis said as they reached their cars.

"Thanks. I'll talk to you next week." They had a few deals

in different stages and usually touched base at least once or twice a week.

"I'm looking forward to it. Have fun on your date."

"It's not a date!" Isabella said, but Travis had already shut his door and was driving away.

CHAPTER 5

I sabella did treat herself to a pedicure that afternoon. Jen liked to tease her about her pampering ways, but she really didn't go that often, just every other month or so.

On the way home, she stopped by the grocery store to pick up a few things and then went through the local Wendy's drive-thru for a cup of chili. She needed it for the dip she was bringing over to Jen's that evening. Isabella was not a cook, but she did have one good party dish that was crazy simple to make. It was only three ingredients, which was perfect.

When she got home, she pulled out a shallow bowl to make the dip. It was called Prison Food, because it was disgusting to look at, but was delicious. She spread cream cheese along the bottom of the bowl, added the chili, then ripped open a bag of shredded cheddar cheese and sprinkled half over the top. Then, it went into the refrigerator.

She still had a few hours before she needed to head to Jen's, so she decided to have a cup of tea and check her work emails. The time quickly flew by as she found a few new listings had come in that day. Isabella didn't usually take office shifts on the weekends, but the newer agents did and there were always some walk-in customers.

It was a trade-off. By not doing office hours on weekends she did miss an occasional new customer, but at this stage in her career, she didn't mind that so much. Plus, she was always available for showings on the weekends, and had two scheduled for the following day on one of her listings.

Missy was in the office both Saturday and Sunday this weekend and had been excited to take the shifts. So far, she had surprised Isabella with her energy and initiative. One of the showings on her listing the next day was for one of Missy's new clients, a walk-in that had come in earlier that morning while Isabella was at the food pantry.

She kept an eye on the clock and then gave Jolene a small can of food before she took the dip out of the refrigerator and put it into a bag along with a fresh package of tortilla chips, and drove over to Jen's.

Anna was already there when she arrived and was helping Jen in the kitchen. Jen's condo had a gorgeous kitchen—it was all white, and was pretty and homey at the same time. Unlike Isabella, Jen loved to cook, and the kitchen was what sold her. Isabella had known she'd fall in love with it as soon as she laid eyes on it.

Jen was also a bit of a clutter nut and Isabella smiled at the bulging trashcan in the corner of the kitchen. She suspected that her sister had run around before they arrived, scooping up piles of old mail and magazines and other odds and ends that had piled up. Jen had stacks of books, both paper and hardcovers, scattered around the living room.

Isabella handed Jen the dip and chips and folded up the bag she'd brought them over in, tucking it neatly in the trash.

"Oh, great, you made Prison Food! I'm so excited. Haven't had this in ages." Jen uncovered the dip and put it in the microwave for two minutes, to get the cheeses all melted and delicious.

"Help yourself to whatever you feel like drinking. There's wine open and soda in the fridge," Jen added as she grabbed a potholder and pulled a bubbling casserole dish out of the oven. She set it on a large plate and then brought it over to the island where Anna was already sitting and sipping a glass of red wine.

Isabella poured herself a soda water, added a squeeze of lemon, and then sat next to Anna. Jen's creation smelled amazing.

"Is that your artichoke dip?" She thought she recognized the tantalizing smell.

"None other. Dig in. There's some toasted baguette slices and crackers to go with it."

Jen added a bit of red wine to her own glass, and then joined the other two at the island. Just as she was about to sit down, the microwave dinged and she went back for Isabella's dip, bringing it and the chips over to the island as well.

"I figured we can just relax and snack for a while," she said as she settled back onto her stool. "Then later, I have a huge antipasto salad."

"That sounds great," Isabella said, as she scooped a cracker into the artichoke dip and took a bite.

"So, when and where is your next research trip?" Anna asked Jen, who blushed a bit before answering. Anna had been at Jen's party and, along with everyone else, had met Ian, who'd flown in from Ireland to surprise her.

"Well, this most recent book has been really popular, and the readers are demanding a sequel. So, to satisfy them, I guess I need to go back to Ireland and maybe Scotland, too."

"Do you really need to go back, though, since you were just there?" Isabella teased her sister.

"Oh, hush. You know why I want to go back. I can't wait to

see him. It's only been a few weeks since he was here, but it feels like ages." She laughed as she reached for more dip. "Yes, I've got it bad."

Anna sighed, and then took a sip of her wine. She had a sad look in her eyes.

"Are you okay?" Isabella asked.

Anna laughed lightly. "Totally. I was just thinking how wonderful it must be to feel that way about someone. That head-over-heels, can't wait to see them again rush. It's been a long time for me."

Isabella smiled. It was a big step that Anna was even thinking this way. She'd resisted all nudging so far to get 'out there'.

"You'll feel that way again. Maybe it's time to dip your toes in the dating pool?"

A cloudy look passed over Anna's face. She opened her mouth to say something, but then reached for a chip instead. Isabella tried again.

"We'll start slow, just get you out and about. We can have a girls' night out. A good excuse to get dressed up and head into Bozeman. There's a charity event coming up soon to raise money for the local food pantries. I'm on the committee so can get a few extra tickets for us."

"I don't know if I'm ready for that," Anna demurred.

"That does sound like fun," Jen said. "Anna, you'll have a blast. It'll just be us girls, so no pressure. Oh, and you never know, there might be some hot guys there you can at least look at."

"There definitely will be," Isabella confirmed.

"You're right. It's time for me to move on. I think I'm finally ready."

"Great, I'll get the tickets for us tomorrow."

ISABELLA WAS NERVOUS. SHE HAD ABOUT TWENTY MINUTES before Aidan was due to arrive and she still hadn't settled on what to wear. She quickly tried a few things on and then settled on an old favorite: a simple, sleeveless black dress with a hot pink cashmere sweater and a vibrant silk scarf that was a mix of pinks and blues. Aidan seemed drawn to bright colors; maybe if things went right, he'd be drawn to her.

Just as she was applying a final coat of lipstick, she heard a car pull into the driveway and then a knock on the door. She ran a brush through her hair one last time and then went downstairs to let him in.

"Hi, Aidan." He stood there looking the part of the successful artist. He was wearing faded designer jeans, a snug fitting black t-shirt and a charcoal gray blazer. His sunny, blonde hair was pulled back in a short ponytail and around his neck, he wore an intriguing brown leather necklace with a dangling shark tooth wrapped in silver.

"You look great!" He leaned in to give her a hug. "Are you almost ready to go?"

"I'm ready. I just need to get my bag." She grabbed her purse off the kitchen table and then followed Aidan out the door.

He opened the passenger side door of an oversized, white jeep that had a rental tag on it. Isabella climbed in and pulled the door shut.

"Looks like you need to buy a car, too," she commented.

Aidan laughed. "I do. That's next on the list. I might actually get one of these. It was all they had left at the rental place when I flew in and I'm surprised by how much I like it."

They chatted easily as Aidan drove to the art gallery in Bozeman. When they arrived and were walking towards the door, Aidan looked a bit nervous and said, "By the way, thank you for agreeing to come with me at the last minute. I hate going to these things and being the center of attention. It always helps to have a friend along."

"I was happy to come. I love art, and have been curious to see what all the fuss is about." She teased him to lighten the mood and help him to relax. "You'll do a great job. Don't worry," she added with a smile.

There was a good crowd gathered already, people sipping cocktails and wandering around exploring Aidan's many paintings that were displayed on easels and hung on the wall. When they walked in, a hush fell over the room and the air was thick with anticipation.

A small, older man with wispy, gray hair and thick glasses came rushing over to greet them.

"I can't believe you're finally here! I've been wanting to show you off for so long." He wrapped Aidan in a bear hug and then glanced at Isabella.

"Rudy, this is Isabella. She's an old friend who was kind enough to join me this evening."

"A very pretty old friend, I must say. A pleasure to meet you." Rudy held out his hand and Isabella went to shake it, but he instead lifted it to his lips for a dramatic kiss.

"Now, come in, come in, both of you. Everyone is eager to meet the artist."

Rudy led Aidan to the front of the room where there was a step up to a small platform with a microphone. The crowd of about a hundred and fifty art-lovers gathered around. Isabella followed along as well and stood off to the side as Aidan was introduced and then took the mic to say a few words of appreciation. After a robust round of applause, he made his way back to her and they walked around the room, pausing by each painting as Aidan gave her a little background history about each one. They were interrupted constantly by people coming over to say hello and to ask questions or, more commonly, to tell him how much they loved his work. Isabella was impressed; he was extremely talented and had a lot of fans.

The few hours they spent there flew by and when the last guest had left, Rudy insisted on taking them to his favorite neighborhood restaurant, a small, family-owned pub that was known for its burgers. Rudy was a charming host and the conversation was lively. They all had the burgers and split a piece of delicious chocolate cake three ways as it was massive. Isabella was quite surprised to learn that both Aidan and Rudy were avid kayakers.

"I just joined a local kayak club," Aidan told them. "There's a river trip coming up in a few weeks that should be a good time." He turned to Isabella. "I think your sister is a member, isn't she?"

"She is. She tried to get me to go to on yesterday's trip, but I was busy. It sounded fun, though. I might go on a future trip," she surprised herself by saying.

"You should, it's a blast. Come on the next one."

"Maybe I will." Suddenly, kayaking seemed a whole lot more interesting.

"Well, this old man needs to get home," Rudy said as he pushed himself up from the table. "It's way past my bedtime," he joked.

Isabella was surprised to see that it was nearly ten. They'd been at the pub for several hours and the time had flown.

On the way back to Beauville, they chatted about the house and the timeline for all the things that needed to be done.

"I have to say, I'm really proud of Missy. She seems so on top of things. I think she's going to do well," Aidan said.

Isabella had to agree. Missy was certainly off to a good

start. She was very organized and made sure that Aidan was updated on everything.

Aidan pulled into Isabella's condo complex, parked and then walked her to the door.

"Thanks again for coming with me. It was a great night." He pulled her in for a quick hug and Isabella was a little disappointed that it didn't last but a second.

"It was fun for me, too. Thank you for bringing me. I enjoyed seeing your work and it's really amazing."

Aidan wasn't comfortable with compliments.

"Thanks, that means a lot to me. So, I guess I'll see you kayaking real soon?"

Isabella laughed, "You just might."

CHAPTER 6

"So, I keep the kayak tied up down here at the pond. No need to lug it around if I don't have to." Uncle Jim led Isabella to the small pond behind his house. He'd been thrilled when she called at lunch to see if he'd mind if she borrowed his kayak after all, and had suggested she stop by after work for a quick lesson.

"You can come by whenever you want to get it, and I'm in no hurry to get it back. You'll need some muscle, though, and a bigger car to carry it.

"Thanks, I'll see who I can round up."

They reached the water's edge and there was the kayak. It was a bright yellow, single-seater model.

"Okay, watch and learn. I'll show you and then you can jump in." Uncle Jim gingerly stepped into the water, and then into the kayak and used one of the oars to push off.

"See? Nothing to it." He paddled around a bit, then came back the edge and got out, splashing into the shallow water.

Isabella was wearing shorts as she expected to get wet, and had on a pair of rubbery crocs so she wouldn't feel whatever she had to step on. She managed to climb into the kayak and looked back at Uncle Jim.

"Okay, you're in! Now grab that oar and push off, then use both of them to steer yourself where you want to go."

She did as he suggested and had to admit, it was kind of fun to be floating around. Kayaking didn't seem that hard at all.

She paddled around for about ten minutes, then headed back to where Uncle Jim was waiting at the water's edge. When she stepped out, he grabbed the rope from the front of the kayak and tied it to the end of his make-shift dock.

"You looked good out there. Fun, right?"

"Yes, it is fun, and easier than I thought it would be."

"Well, keep in mind this is just a little pond. It's a bit trickier on those rivers. You have to really pay attention."

"I will."

"I'm glad you're giving it a go. Good for you to try something different," Uncle Jim said as they walked back to the house.

"Something smells wonderful," Isabella said as they stepped into the kitchen.

"It's a spice cake. One of those box mixes. Your sister showed me how to make them a few months ago and it's easier than I thought."

The timer dinged a few minutes later, and Uncle Jim put on two oven mitts and pulled a large, rectangular baking pan out of the oven and set it on the stove. Isabella was amused to see that stacked next to the stove was a tower of cake mix boxes, all different flavors, nearly a dozen of them.

"Did they have a sale on cake mix?" she asked.

"Ten for a dollar. You can't beat that."

"No, that is a deal," Isabella agreed.

"We can eat now, and have cake for dessert. You're okay

with hot dogs and beans?"

"Of course."

Uncle Jim grilled up the hot dogs and toasted the buns while Isabella warmed a can of beans on the stove. Then they sat outside on his screened-in porch to enjoy the meal.

"How's that new girl working out? Missy? You still training her?" Uncle Jim asked before he took a bite of beans.

"She's on her own now, but I'm still there if she has any questions."

"Ethel Maxwell is going to be giving you a call this week. She wants to sell her place now that Harry's gone. Going to move into Bozeman, closer to her kids."

"Ethel is the brown house at the end of this street, right?" Isabella didn't know Ethel well but as long as she could remember, she'd been one of Uncle Jim's neighbors. Her husband Harry had passed away almost two years ago.

"Yeah, saw her at the Muffin yesterday morning and we got to chatting." His face darkened and he looked as though he was debating what to say. Finally, the words spilled out. "She told me she was going to sell and that she was planning to call Missy to list the house. Said she knew Missy's mom and wanted to try and help Missy out. I set her straight on that."

"You did? What did you say?" Isabella was both amused and grateful that Uncle Jim was so indignant on her behalf.

"Well, I just reminded her that she'd been my neighbor forever and that you're the best realtor in Beauville and if she wanted her house sold right, she needed to call you."

"Thank you." This time Uncle Jim was there to intervene, but Isabella realized this scenario was likely to happen again. Missy was well-liked in town and although she was new to selling real estate, she knew a lot of people and they were rooting for her to do well.

Missy had brought a new client in earlier that week that

Isabella also knew. The Weavers were a young couple who recently had a second child and wanted to upgrade to a larger home. Christine Weaver was a friend of her sister, Jen, and if Missy wasn't in the picture, they would likely have called her. But, Missy and Christine were also friends. Beauville was a small town, so it was bound to happen. The only good thing was that she'd at least get a piece of the sale if Missy found them a house.

"Business still good?" Uncle Jim asked and Isabella sensed that he was worried about her losing clients to Missy. Isabella wasn't worried, though; not yet, anyway.

"Yes, it's all good. Busy as ever."

"DID HE ASK YOU TO GO KAYAKING?" JEN ASKED AS THE waitress dropped off a round of drinks at their table. It was Thursday night and Isabella, Anna and Jen were at the food pantry's charity event in Bozeman, and had just settled themselves at one of the only remaining empty tables.

"Sort of," Isabella replied as she took a sip of her soda water and lemon.

"What does that mean, exactly?"

"Well, he said he was going kayaking soon and that he thought you were part of the group that was going and he suggested I go, too."

"With him?" Jen looked pleased and Isabella knew her answer would disappoint.

"No. Just in general, that I should go."

"Okay, well that's possibly something, I suppose. Has he called you?"

"No." Isabella frowned as doubt washed over her. "Maybe this isn't such a good idea after all."

"Are you kidding? That you even considered going is huge. I never thought I'd get you into a kayak. We are going, and I'm going to hold you to it."

"Did I just hear you say you're going kayaking? I must have misheard, right?" Travis was suddenly by their table, sipping a beer and looking both amused and professional in a sharp black suit and red tie.

"Join us for a drink," Jen invited and Travis settled in a chair next to Isabella.

"Ladies, nice to see you all." He glanced around the table and Isabella introduced him to Anna.

"I'm not sure if you've met Anna before. She is our office manager, and one of my best friends."

"Great to meet you, Anna. I know we've talked on the phone." Travis reached across the table to shake her hand.

"I didn't know you were coming to this." Isabella was surprised to see Travis there. She couldn't recall seeing him at any of the previous fundraising events.

"Christian mentioned it a few days ago and said he had an extra ticket if I was interested. I wasn't, really, until he said it was for the food pantry."

"Are Christian and Molly here, too?" She hadn't noticed them yet, but the room was crowded.

"No. They were planning on it, but something came up and he gave his tickets away."

"You two don't mind if I steal Anna away for a minute? I see someone I want to introduce her to." Jen stood and motioned for Anna to follow her, and a moment later they were gone.

"I've always liked your sister," Travis said with a look of amusement.

"Yeah, she's great," Isabella agreed and Travis chuckled.

"So, is it true?"

"Is what true?" Isabella wasn't sure what he was talking about or why he was so amused.

"You, kayaking."

"Oh, yeah, maybe. I told Jen I'd go."

"Have you ever been before?"

Isabella smiled. "Yes, for about ten minutes. On Uncle Jim's pond. It seemed pretty easy."

Travis frowned at that. "You've never gone in a river before?"

"No, why? Is it much harder?"

"It can be, depending on the conditions. Dangerous, even. Do you know how to roll?"

"How to what?"

"Roll your kayak."

"No, why would I do that?"

"In case you flip over. It's a safety move you need to know if you're going on a river."

"Oh." Isabella was starting to reconsider the whole idea of kayaking. No wonder her first instinct had been to avoid it.

"When is the outing?" Travis tapped his finger against the tablecloth. It was a nervous habit he had when he was thinking about something. Isabella had noticed him do it before in his office, when they'd been discussing different legal issues and deciding between options.

"It's next weekend, Sunday afternoon."

"Okay, so we have to do this on Saturday. Plan on at least three to four hours. I'll pick you up at nine and we can swing by your Uncle Jim's to get the kayak."

Isabella hesitated. "I don't know about this. Can't Jen just show me if we get there a little early on Sunday?" She was feeling apprehensive in general and especially about spending hours with Travis learning how to roll, whatever that meant. She wasn't sure she wanted to know.

"No, there won't be enough time. Trust me, you don't want to be out there without knowing a few basic safety moves."

Isabella wanted to say that she didn't want to be out there period, but instead asked, "So where do we go to learn this? The river?"

"I have a membership at a club in Bozeman. They have a huge indoor pool and leave it open for kayak practice on Saturday mornings. It's the best way to learn how to roll, under controlled conditions so you can master the move."

"Do we really need three or four hours to learn it?" It didn't sound like the best way to spend her Saturday morning, but still she did appreciate that Travis was willing to train her.

"At least. It's not easy. We'll go over other basic stuff, too, so you really know what you are doing."

"Why are you doing this? You must have better ways to spend your weekend."

Travis chuckled and a spray of laugh lines danced around his eyes. "Honestly, not lately. I've worked the past few weekends. But it's getting back to normal now and I'm overdue to get in the kayak. It's one of my favorite ways to relax and unwind, do a little fishing."

"Well, I don't want to put you out." Isabella was still feeling very much on the fence.

"You're not putting me out at all. It'll be fun, I promise. I'm a good teacher." He grinned at her then and she relaxed a bit. Maybe it wouldn't be so bad and if she was going to go with Jen and the others, she could definitely use the practice. Jen probably took it for granted that she was all set.

"So, how was your date with the town's celebrity artist?" Travis's tone was teasing.

"It wasn't really a date," Isabella admitted.

"No?" Travis raised his eyebrows and looked surprised.

"He just wanted someone to go with him to his showing.

Missy was going to go initially, but Jeremy's parents wanted to have them over to dinner, so I went instead."

"Kind of sounds like a date to me." Travis said and then changed the subject. "I'm starving. Want to check out the appetizer table?"

"Sure."

They made their way to a buffet table along the wall that was loaded with all kinds of nibbles: mozzarella cheese and pesto, tomato and basil, shrimp cocktail, various cheese and crackers, assorted dips and so on. They were filling up their plates when Jen and Anna joined them.

The four of them had just sat back down at their table when Travis's phone buzzed. He pulled it out of a pocket, glanced at the number and then said, "I need to step outside and take this. Be right back."

As soon as he walked away, Jen said, "You two looked thick as thieves. Anything going on I should know about?"

"With Travis? Hardly. He's going to help me with some basic kayak moves; how to roll, that kind of thing."

"You don't know how to do that? Jeez, I just assumed. Guess I should have known better. I'm sorry." Jen looked worried.

"Don't be silly. You've had a lot on your mind."

"Does he know the real reason for your sudden interest in kayaking?" Anna asked as she stabbed a mozzarella ball with her fork.

"Aidan? I don't think so. I didn't mention it," Isabella said as Travis returned to the table looking irritated and apologetic.

"I have to take off. Just had a meeting pushed to tomorrow morning and have a mountain of paperwork I need to get through tonight." He turned to Isabella. "I'll see you Saturday at nine."

CHAPTER 7

Isabella arrived at the office the next morning a half-hour earlier than usual, so she could enjoy a cup of coffee with Anna before the rest of the office rolled in and the day got underway. People tended to come in a little later on Fridays as a rule.

"Perfect timing, coffee's ready." Anna smiled as Isabella walked in the door.

"Great, I'll be right in."

Isabella set her bag down and then joined Anna in the conference room.

"I don't know how you do it. It was hard to get up this morning." Anna laughed as she slid a mug of steaming coffee toward Isabella.

"Thanks." Isabella settled into one of the comfy leather chairs and then added, "We weren't even out late. What time did we get home? I think it was around ten thirty?"

"That's late for me, during the week, anyway. I know you're used to it."

"I really don't go out that much. Not lately, anyway. You had fun though, right?"

Anna smiled. "I did. It was nice to get dressed up and go out to something like that, to go anywhere, really, that isn't a kid's game or something kid-related. It felt good."

"We need to do it more often, even if it's something local and low-key, just get out for a girls' night."

"That sounds great to me. Tom's mother said she's always open to watching the boys. She was thrilled to come over last night."

"Good, it's settled then. I'll talk to Jen and we'll make a plan for next week, maybe do Friday night so we can sleep in a little the next day."

"Perfect."

"So, who was it that Jen wanted to introduce you to last night?" Isabella was curious, and neither had mentioned it when they'd returned to the table and Isabella hadn't wanted to push.

Anna looked confused for a moment and then chuckled, "No one. Jen just said that as an excuse for the two of us to leave you and Travis alone together."

"Oh. She didn't need to do that." Jennifer was such a match-maker.

"She thinks you look good together. So do I, actually. Travis seems like a nice guy. Very cute, too. I'm surprised you never mentioned much about him before."

"There's nothing to mention. We go way back, to middle school, actually. He was annoying back then. Now he's just kind of grouchy and bossy. But he is a very good lawyer."

Anna looked thoughtful. "You do a lot of work with him. I suppose that could be awkward if you were to date and then things didn't work out."

"Exactly. That's probably one of the reasons why it's never crossed my mind. Plus, he had a long-term girlfriend for years, and then I was dating Christian, until recently."

"Not that recently. That ended almost a year ago, and it was never that serious."

Isabella opened her mouth to protest and Anna cut her off. "I'm just saying, I doubt Christian would mind if you dated Travis, so that shouldn't stop you."

Isabella chuckled. "Honestly, I just don't think of him that way. I'd really love to get to know Aidan better."

Anna sighed, and then said, "I know, you've had a crush on him for years. But, he's been away a long time. It's almost like he's a stranger."

Isabella had actually thought the same thing. She'd enjoyed spending time with him at the art gallery opening, but if she was being truthful, he was hard to read and it was difficult to tell if he was interested at all or just being friendly.

"He was gone for a long time. Eight years. It's probably an adjustment being back." She grinned. "I'd like to help him settle in."

Anna smiled at that. "I know you would, and you'll be seeing him this weekend, so that's something."

Isabella took a sip of coffee and glanced at her watch. She could sit and chat with Anna all morning, but it was probably about time for her to head to her desk.

"Missy's here early again," Anna commented as the front door opened and the sound of high heels clattered down the hall way.

"How do you know that's her?" Isabella asked.

"Easy enough. No one else wears heels every day. You do occasionally but you're already accounted for. She seems to be making quite an impression."

"That she does. Dottie gave the green light yesterday for her to be on call rotation, though I'm sure you know that already." This meant that Missy had her blessing to handle new, incoming clients, people who walked in or called on an ad.

"She also mentioned to me when she left yesterday she has another new client coming in today. Some cousin that just divorced and moved back here from Texas or Alabama—I forget which, but somewhere in the deep South."

"No kidding? She really is getting off to a fast start." Isabella was impressed and, for the first time, felt a stir of competitiveness towards the new realtor.

ISABELLA ARRIVED BACK IN THE OFFICE A FEW MINUTES PAST ONE and had about twenty minutes before her next appointment, just enough time to eat the takeout salad she'd picked up from the Morning Muffin. She settled at her desk, opened her email and started eating lunch while keeping an eye on the time. Her next appointment was an initial meeting with a young married couple, first-time buyers who were both nervous and excited to find a house they could afford.

Missy was eating a sandwich at her desk and glancing at the clock every few minutes as well. Just as Isabella was finishing her salad, she heard the front door open and there was no mistaking the sound of high heels. Isabella doubted that this was her buyers. Not many people wore heels in Beauville unless they were attached to cowboy boots.

Sure enough, a minute later, Missy's phone rang. Isabella guessed it was Francie at the front desk, calling to let her know her client was in the reception area as Missy was only on the phone for a second before jumping up and heading to the main entrance. About five minutes later she was back, with a tall, very pretty woman who looked to be in her early thirties. She had lots of long, layered hair that was very blonde and arranged in a froth of fluffy waves. Her eyes were blue and she had a cute, turned-up nose that bore a slight resemblance to Missy's. Her lipstick was a very bright pinky-red and matched her high heels perfectly. She was the picture perfect vision of a Southern Belle.

"Isabella, this is my cousin, Bethany Evans. She just moved home from Atlanta."

"Nice to meet you." Isabella wondered how long Bethany had been away from Beauville. She didn't remember her at all.

"Bethany lived in Bozeman until she got married ten years ago. She and Bill met in college and his family lives in Atlanta," Missy explained.

"I heard that it's lovely there, and warm," Isabella said with a smile. She'd never been to Atlanta and imagined that coming home might be an adjustment after living in a big city for so long.

"It's hot as hell and I don't care if I ever go back," Bethany snapped, then immediately looked slightly contrite. "Sorry, I recently went through an exhausting divorce and just wanted to get out of there and not look back."

"Her parents moved to Beauville a few years ago, so Bethany was thinking she might want to rent a condo nearby and maybe eventually buy something, but for now just rent."

Isabella mentally ran through their current inventory of rentals.

They had a few available condos that were basic two bedrooms and one more upscale townhouse that had soaring cathedral ceilings, a light-filled loft and gorgeous granite in the kitchen and bathrooms. It was Isabella's listing and was also in her condo complex and was a mirror image of her own unit, just at the opposite end of the building.

"Have you looked through any of the listings yet?" she asked Missy.

"Yes, I told Bethany about all three. She only wants to see your listing."

Of course she did.

"It's vacant now, so we can look at it this afternoon if you like. I have an appointment in a few minutes, but should be free in about a half-hour if you want to go then."

"That's perfect," Missy said. "Bethany and I have a lot to catch up on. We can go grab coffee and then be back then."

ISABELLA WAS JUST SAYING GOOD-BYE TO THE PETERSONS, HER newly married buyers, when Missy and Bethany strolled back in to the office. They quickly turned around and Isabella followed them outside and drove them to look at the townhouse rental.

"I have to say, for a small town, there are some cute men here," Bethany drawled as Isabella parked the car and they got out.

No one said anything, so she continued talking, "Missy took me to that Muffin shop so we could chat a bit and there were some impressive-looking men that came and went while we were there. Not that I'm looking, of course, but I'm not blind either."

"A few people we knew came in to get lunch to go," Missy said. "She got to meet both Aidan and Travis."

"Really? They both came in? That's odd." Isabella was surprised.

"Not really. Aidan doesn't cook, so he gets lunch there almost every day and Travis's office is right across the street, and we were there at lunchtime."

"True, it's not like there're many options here in Beauville," Isabella agreed.

"It's a nice change from Atlanta. I knew tons of people there and hardly ever ran into anyone." Bethany pulled a lipstick out of her purse and reapplied as they walked toward the door. "I didn't expect to meet people so soon."

"Well, there's no one here, so you can take your time looking around," Isabella said as she unlocked the front door and they stepped inside.

"It's a furnished unit, too?" Bethany asked as she looked around the inviting living room and its oversized, cream-colored sofa.

"Yes, this unit is fully furnished. The owners are spending a year abroad. The husband's company has an office in London."

They walked around the townhouse and Isabella had no doubt that Bethany would want the unit. It was beautifully furnished and when she heard a squeal coming from the over-sized walk-in closet in the master bedroom, she knew it was a done deal.

"Looks like we're going to be neighbors," Bethany confirmed in her annoyingly sugary drawl when she and Missy finished their tour.

"Great. I'll get the paperwork started." Her client would be thrilled that they'd found a renter so quickly. Isabella wasn't sure if she was quite as enthusiastic about her soon to be new neighbor.

CHAPTER 8

Isabella woke earlier than usual on Saturday morning. She was a little nervous about her kayaking adventure with Travis.

"Jolene, what have I gotten myself into?" The little cat purred and rubbed against her leg as she spooned cat food into a small bowl and then set it down for her.

After having a yogurt and just one cup of coffee, she went upstairs to get ready. She chose her most modest swimsuit, a deep chocolate brown one-piece with a simple scoop neck. She wouldn't have to worry about anything falling out of place in that suit and figured her mind would definitely be elsewhere trying to learn whatever it was Travis was determined to teach her.

At nine o'clock sharp, there was a knock at the door.

When she opened it, Travis stood there, looking decidedly more energetic and excited than Isabella thought the occasion warranted.

"You ready to go?"

"As ready as I'll ever be," she said with chuckle as she grabbed her purse and followed Travis out the door. She climbed into the passenger side of his truck and he drove to Uncle Jim's to pick up the kayak. When they arrived, she saw that Uncle Jim was waiting for them outside on his screened-in porch and that he had company. He stood and motioned them in as Travis parked the car.

"Look who came to see me!" Molly's mother and Aunt Betty were sitting around the table, drinking coffee and eating something sweet. "I told the girls if they came to visit, I'd make a coffee cake just for them."

"Nice to see you, Isabella, and Travis," Molly's mother said politely.

"Where are the two of you off to?" Aunt Betty asked with interest. She was up on all the town gossip and took pride in being the first to know what going on. Isabella was about to answer when Uncle Jim jumped in. "The kids are going kayaking. Travis is going to give her a lesson before she hits the river tomorrow with a group of people."

"Jen is in a kayaking club," Isabella added.

"Are you in the club, too?" Aunt Betty asked Travis.

"No, I'm just giving Isabella a few pointers."

"I see," Aunt Betty said as she reached over and cut herself another thick slice of cake.

"Would you like to join us?" Molly's mom invited. She was very sweet and much quieter than Aunt Betty.

"It looks delicious, but we should probably get going," Isabella answered.

"Come on, then. I'll take you down to the kayak and then you two can be on your way." Uncle Jim started walking toward the water and they followed close behind. Travis easily picked up the kayak and carried it back to the truck where he slid it in the back, next to his own red one. They said goodbye to Uncle Jim and then headed to Bozeman.

The athletic club was quiet when they arrived a half-hour later. Travis brought their kayaks inside and dropped them both into one end of the huge swimming pool.

"Are you ready to do this?" Travis asked as he stripped off his t-shirt. Isabella was speechless for a moment. Who knew he was hiding abs like that? Travis was very fit and both his arms and abs had clearly defined muscles. She felt a bit self-conscious as she pulled off her own white t-shirt and slipped off her shorts.

"Okay, jump in." Travis dove in head first and then watched as Isabella dipped her toes in the water and then slowly eased herself in. The water wasn't cold, and actually felt nice as her body got used to it.

They spent the first hour practicing how to get in and out of the kayak from the water which wasn't so easy to do, but eventually Isabella got the hang of it.

"Okay, now you're ready to learn how to roll," Travis said. He then went on to explain how the move was done and how she needed to use her hips to swing the boat over and then back up. It sounded difficult to Isabella and it was. But they kept at it for several hours and eventually, she mastered it and then learned a few other safety maneuvers. Finally, Travis said they were done. Isabella was exhausted but also very glad that he had taken the time to show her things. She felt much better now about tackling the river and realized how little she'd known.

They dragged the kayaks to the shallow end of the pool and Travis climbed out first, lifting his kayak behind him. Isabella followed as Travis jumped back in to get her kayak as well. She took two steps up and then lost her footing and started to slip. Travis immediately caught her, wrapping his arms around her middle and lifting her back up. His touch was unexpected and caught her by surprise. He held on a moment longer until she found her footing and then eased up.

"Thank you." Isabella stepped out of the pool and then watched as Travis pulled her kayak out, admiring his body again as he moved and his muscles flexed. He was bigger and stronger than he looked in his suit and his arms had felt nice wrapped around her. She shook off the thought, though. It was just that it had been awhile since she had felt any arms around her. She dried off with a towel and then put her clothes back on. Travis did the same and brought the kayaks back to the truck.

"I owe you lunch, at least," Isabella said once they were both back in the truck.

"I won't say no to a sandwich," Travis said with a grin as he started the engine.

THEY RODE BACK TO BEAUVILLE AND CHATTED EASILY, MOSTLY about work as they had several deals pending at different stages. Travis had a hard time keeping his mind focused on work matters, though. He was distracted by the image of Isabella in her swimsuit that kept replaying in his mind. It was a modest suit but it couldn't hide her curves, and if Travis was being truthful, he would have to admit that he'd kept his arms around her a minute longer than he needed to. He just hadn't wanted to let go of her softness and her sweet scent that he wanted to lose himself in. He was starting to wonder if he was kidding himself, though. Isabella had never shown the slightest sign of attraction to him. His stomach growled then and snapped him out of his thoughts as he also realized she had just asked him a question.

"I'm sorry, what was that?"

"I was just asking if the Muffin was okay?"

"Perfect," he agreed as he turned the truck onto Main Street and then a moment later found a spot to park. It was nearly two by then so the lunch rush had quieted down and just a few minutes after placing their orders at the counter, their food was ready. They both ordered sandwiches; rare roast beef for Isabella and turkey piled high on an onion roll for Travis.

"First time I've seen you eat something other than salad for lunch," Travis observed once they'd settled at a table, and Isabella laughed.

"I'm starving! We worked up an appetite."

"Yes, we did." Travis forced his mind not to return to the image of Isabella in her wet bathing suit. He tore open a bag of chips and picked up his sandwich.

They were just about done eating when Travis heard a slightly familiar voice and noticed Isabella stiffen. Moments later, the same pretty blonde woman he'd met the day before was standing by their table.

"Travis, right?" she asked, and then glanced at Isabella as if surprised to see her there. "And nice to see you again, Isabella. What are you two up to?"

"Just having lunch," Isabella answered flatly.

"We were kayaking in Bozeman," Travis explained.

"Kayaking, how adventurous." She narrowed her gaze at Isabella. "I wouldn't have guessed you were into that."

"Just trying something new." Isabella smiled, but Travis noticed that it was a tight smile and didn't light up her face like it usually would have.

"Well, I won't keep you. Just wanted to say hi. I stopped in to get some bagels for tomorrow's breakfast." She flashed a brilliant smile Travis's way and then sashayed out the door.

"That's some accent she has. We don't see too many Southerners here," he commented as he reached for the last bite of his sandwich.

"Her accent is fake," Isabella snapped, and then after a moment she explained. "Bethany grew up in Bozeman and then went to college in the South and stayed there after graduating and getting married."

"No kidding? I guess I wouldn't know the difference between a real or fake Southern accent, then."

"No, I don't suppose you would. How could you?" Isabella agreed.

They dropped off Isabella's kayak after lunch. Uncle Jim wasn't home, so they just left it by the side porch so she and Jen could grab it in the morning.

Travis wondered what Isabella was up to that evening, if she had a date. He hoped not, and couldn't help asking as he pulled into the visitor spot by her condo.

"So, any big plans tonight?"

"Not really. Jen and I talked about maybe seeing a movie."

"That's a good idea. I imagine you're leaving early tomorrow?"

"Too early for my liking," Isabella said. "Jen is picking me up a little after seven and then we have to get the kayak and meet everyone at the river by eight."

"You'll do fine," he assured her. "Just remember to have fun."

Isabella smiled. "I'll try to remember that, and thank you for everything. I really appreciate it."

"It was nothing."

Sunday morning was clear and sunny, and Jen was full of

energy, chatting away as Isabella climbed into her SUV and they drove to Uncle Jim's to get the kayak. He wasn't up yet, so they quickly dragged the kayak to Jen's car and loaded it in next to her bright blue one. As they drove to the river, Jen gave her the low down on how the day would unfold. They would drop in at the meeting site and then kayak down river for about four hours, then have a cook-out lunch together. Then shuttles would be waiting to bring them and their kayaks back to their cars.

"Don't be nervous. You'll do great and I'll stick right by you," Jen assured her as they parked and together carried each kayak over to where their group was beginning to gather.

"How many people are coming?" Isabella asked.

"I think there will be about twenty all together, and all levels, too, from beginners to more advanced."

Ten minutes later, a bright red jeep pulled in to the lot. Aidan bounced out and pulled his sleek, black kayak from the back and carried it over to the water's edge. When he turned, he saw Jen and Isabella and came over to them.

"Nice to see some familiar faces. Are you both looking forward to this?"

"We did this run last year and it's a great route. You'll love it," Jen said.

"I'm a little nervous," Isabella admitted. "It's my first river ride."

"No kidding? You are in for a treat. It's addicting, a rush. You'll see," Aidan said as their group leader called them to attention and began to explain how they would proceed. Once he finished, everyone lined up and dropped their kayaks in the water one by one and pushed out into the river. The water was calm in this spot so it made for a good loading area. Isabella followed Jen, and once they were all in the water, the group leader paddled to the head of the group and waved for everyone to head downstream.

The next few hours alternated between exhilaration and terror for Isabella as she struggled to stay upright when they hit the rough sections. Jen kept an eye on her and Isabella kept her attention focused on mirroring what Jen was doing as they approached each new area of the river.

She almost lost it at one point when she saw another kayak flip over and turned to look. Out of the corner of her eye, she was relieved to see kayaker quickly regain their balance as they rolled back into position. Isabella took a deep breath and focused on staying steady and trying to enjoy the ride. She did actually enjoy the smooth parts when they floated along through calmer waters, and once she made it through some of the rougher patches she realized that they had been fun, too, almost like a roller coaster ride as they went through some areas that dropped down quickly or curved around corners.

Finally, they reached their end point and were once again in a calm, slow-moving pool of water where everyone glided to the shore and pulled their kayaks out. One of the group organizers already had a grill going and Isabella could smell hotdogs and hamburgers cooking. They carried their kayaks to the waiting shuttles and loaded them in, then made their way to a tent and found seats at one of the picnic tables after helping themselves to sodas. Moments later, someone hollered that the food was ready and they loaded their plates with hotdogs, burgers, potato salad and chips.

"I can't believe I'm having one of each," Isabella said as they sat down with their food.

Jen's own plate was identical, as was Aidan's when he joined them.

"So, what did you think?" Aidan asked.

"It was fun," Isabella admitted.

"Fun enough to do again?"

"Maybe." She hadn't thought that far ahead.

"There's another trip coming up in two weeks, you have to come. That one is even better, and longer. It goes all day. You'll love it."

Isabella wasn't sure how she wanted to respond to that, so she opted to take a bite of her hot dog instead and to change the subject.

"So, Aidan, are you excited for next week?" He was due to close on his house the following Wednesday.

"Yes, I can't wait to move in. I don't think Aunt Edna is looking forward to it, though. She likes having me around."

"At least you'll be close by." His new house was just a few miles down the road from where his Aunt lived.

"I know, I keep reminding her of that."

"How does it feel to be back?" Jen asked.

"It's good. In some ways, it's like I never left, even though it's been years. Things haven't changed much here." He paused to take a bite of his burger and then continued. "Didn't there used to be a big music and art festival around this time of year?"

"You mean the Sweet Pea Festival?" Isabella asked.

"Yes, that sounds right."

"It's next weekend, I think," Jen said.

"And it's bigger and better now," Isabella added. "It's really grown over the years. They always have top musicians and artists. You should go."

"I was thinking I'd want to check it out. Do you want to join me?" Aidan asked, and then added, "Both of you. It sounds like a good time."

"We'd love to. We go every year." Isabella was thrilled that he'd asked, even if it was a general invite for the both of them.

Jen hesitated before saying, "I'm not sure if I can make it, but you two should definitely go and have a blast."

"Great, I'll plan on it and touch base with you next week. It goes all weekend so maybe we should go Friday night and then head back Saturday or Sunday if we want."

Isabella agreed and then smiled all the way home. It had turned out to be a very good

CHAPTER 9

Missy was excited about her first closing, and as she and Isabella pulled into the parking lot by Travis's office, she admitted that she was a little nervous, too.

"At this point, there's nothing to be nervous about. This is the easy part. It's just the signing of a stack of legal documents and exchange of money. Aidan will be a homeowner and you'll have completed your first sale," Isabella assured her as they walked up the stairs to Travis's office on the second floor.

"Good morning, girls," Mrs. Crosby welcomed them and then brought them into a conference room. "Can I get coffee for either of you?"

"No, thank you." Isabella and Missy both said at once.

"I'll let Travis know that you're both here."

Isabella and Missy settled into soft, brown leather chairs that were around a large, oval table. Isabella had been in this room many times for closings. It was a warm, welcoming space, with brick walls and a gas fireplace in one corner and paintings of Montana's mountains and country-sides along the wall.

Aidan arrived a few minutes later and sat next to Missy.

"Will you move in right away?" Missy asked.

"As soon as I can, but probably not for a week or so. I don't have any furniture and may want to do some painting. I'm not sure about that. I need to get a closer look at the walls and then decide."

"That sounds like fun, the shopping for furniture part," Missy said.

"You think so? I'm not sure if fun is the word I'd use." Aidan laughed, then added, "I'd love your help with that, actually."

Before Missy could answer, Travis entered the room with a stack of papers under one arm. He was followed by an older man that Isabella didn't recognize.

"Hi, everyone. This is Neil Johnson, the seller's lawyer."

"Are the sellers going to be here, too?" Missy asked.

"No, they opted not to be. Mr. Johnson will be handling everything on their behalf."

The two men sat down and then the signing of legal documents began. An hour later, the process finished with the exchange of a cashier's check and a ring of keys to the house. Mr. Johnson departed as the others prepared to do the same. They were all about to walk out of the conference room when Travis turned to Isabella and asked, "I meant to ask earlier, how was your kayak trip?"

"It was fun, I managed to stay upright the whole time," Isabella said with a laugh.

"She did great," Aidan added.

Travis's eyes narrowed at that. "You were there?"

"There was a big group of us. I was glad to see Isabella go. I'd encouraged her to do it a few weeks ago."

"I see." Travis's voice had a chill to it that Isabella wasn't used to.

"That reminds me, too. Are we still on for the festival on Friday?" Aidan looked at Isabella for confirmation.

"Yes, I'm still up for it."

"The two of you are going to the Sweet Pea festival?" Missy sounded surprised, a bit annoyed, even.

"You know I always loved going to that. Do you want to join us?"

Missy was silent for a long moment before finally saying, "Jeremy and I have plans Friday night. Thanks anyway."

"Okay, how about furniture shopping? Can you go tonight or tomorrow night?" he asked Missy.

"You should call Traci, she's really good at that, or maybe Isabella will want to go. This week is crazy for me." Her tone was definitely cool.

Aidan looked at Isabella and seemed unsure as to what he should do.

"I'm happy to help, but I think you'd probably be best with Traci. She's great at helping you decorate so that it looks like you. I'd just be picking out things I like," Isabella smiled.

"Okay, thanks. I'll give her a call." Then he glanced at Missy and added, "If you change your mind, let me know. You know my style and what I like."

When she and Missy were back in the car, Isabella asked, "Is everything okay? How's Jeremy?"

"Everything's fine. Couldn't be better. Jeremy is a sweetheart. I'm very lucky."

———

"You look like you could use one of my raspberry muffins, honey." Mrs. Crosby walked into Travis's office without knocking and set a dish with the muffin and a cup of freshly brewed hot coffee on his desk.

"Thank you." He smiled back at her, but she still looked worried.

"Everything is fine," he assured her. "I'm just thinking about a million things. You know how it is."

"Well, slow down a bit and enjoy the muffin. It should cheer you up." And with that, she was gone, back to her desk out front, and Travis was left with his dark mood. He'd felt furious when he'd heard that Aidan was the reason Isabella went kayaking in the first place. And to think he'd helped with that. Clearly, he was a fool and should just look elsewhere, try and get his mind off someone who didn't seem to have even an inkling of interest. He sighed and then broke off a piece of muffin and popped it in his mouth. The sweet, tart flavor of the raspberries did cheer him up, a little. Minutes later, the muffin was history and his bad mood was mostly gone, for the time being.

MISSY WAS IN AN OFF MOOD FOR THE REST OF THE WEEK, SO Isabella just tried to stay out of her way, which wasn't hard because she was busy with showings and new listings and was barely in the office anyway.

Friday afternoon quieted down, finally, around three thirty, and when Isabella stopped back into the office, Missy wasn't there and the place was a ghost town. Bill and Jake were both available to handle any incoming calls or walk-ins, so Isabella was glad she'd decided to take a break. She strolled into Anna's office and handed her one of the paper cups of coffee she'd just picked up at the Muffin.

"Perfect timing, thanks! I was just about to make myself a cup. I don't know where this day has gone," Anna said.

Isabella collapsed into an extra chair next to Anna's desk and took a sip of her own coffee.

"I'm glad it's slowed down a bit. I may take off early today."

"You should. Any particular reason?"

"An email from Snow's, actually. They are having a big sale. I haven't been there in a while." Snow's was the only department store in Beauville and had an especially good shoe section.

"What, it's been over a week?" Anna teased.

"Very funny." Isabella smiled, then asked, "How's Missy been today? Still a grump?"

"Just quiet. Not her usual, perky self."

"I don't know what is going on with her."

"I have a suspicion," Anna said. "I think she's jealous that you're going out with Aidan. Maybe she still has feelings for him."

"Do you really think so? She told me that she's crazy about Jeremy or that he's a really great guy. Something like that."

"Hmmm, well those are two very different things."

"I suppose."

"So, are you excited to be going out with him tonight? It's finally a real date."

Isabella considered that. "Yes, I'm looking forward to it, but he did ask Jen to go, too."

"He was probably just being polite, since you were both there."

"Maybe." Isabella took another sip of coffee and started to relax.

"So, I was thinking," Anna began. "The kids are going to stay with their grandparents next weekend and I thought it might be fun to have a small party. You know I love to cook and I haven't entertained in ages."

Isabella loved the idea. "That would be so fun."

"I was thinking of maybe doing an informal wine tasting, asking everyone to bring a bottle and keep it in the brown paper bag, so we don't know what we're tasting, and then having everyone vote on their favorites."

"I bet people will love that."

"I know you don't usually drink, but you used to like wine, if I recall."

"I still have a glass every now and then. Wine tasting is usually just small sips, right? Maybe I will try a few." Isabella thought the party would be a great way for Anna to ease her way back into being more social and maybe even meeting someone.

"Call me tomorrow and let me know how the date goes tonight. I am living vicariously through you," Anna said with a laugh.

"I can't wait to hear about your dates. You'll be out there soon, I can feel it." Isabella could sense that Anna was finally ready and open to meeting someone.

"Maybe. The thought of it terrifies me a bit. I know that's silly," Anna admitted.

"Not silly at all. Completely normal. Once you start getting out there, it will just happen when it's meant to. Your party is a good step towards that."

They discussed the guest list and possible menu for the next half hour and then Isabella went back to her desk to do a final email check and shut things down for the day.

CHAPTER 10

Isabella always looked forward to the Sweet Pea Festival. As long as she could remember, the festival marked the beginning of the end of summer. It was a beautiful night and she dressed casually, in a favorite pair of well-worn jeans and a flattering, deep pink V-neck sweater. She debated wearing the cute new shoes she'd just picked up at the Snow's sale, but decided against it. They'd be doing a lot of walking around at the festival and she was prone to blisters with new shoes when she did that. Instead, she opted for a pair of soft, leather sandals.

Aidan came by a few minutes past six to pick her up and they headed to Bozeman. The festival was underway and they could hear the music as they pulled in to park.

"There's a country-rock band coming on at eight," Aidan said as they walked toward the gate. "I think right now it's some kind of a dance production. I thought we could check out the art booths first and then catch the band after, if that sounds good to you?"

"Sounds perfect," Isabella agreed as Aidan bought their tickets at the counter and they made their way in.

There was a festive energy in the air as they walked around the grounds, stopping every now and again to visit different art booths. At most of them, Aidan chatted with the artists, while Isabella browsed. There were some very talented artists in the area and the styles varied greatly.

"Would you ever want to do this? Have a booth here?" she asked, once they'd started to move on to the next booth.

"I might. It's exciting to see that there seems to be a vibrant art community here. Most of the folks I've talked to said they are local."

They'd only visited half of the artist booths by the time the band was ready to start playing. As they changed course to walk towards the music, they entered the food area and everything smelled delicious.

"Are you hungry?" Aidan asked.

Isabella's stomach growled and they both laughed. "I guess I am."

"What sounds good to you?" There were lots of vendors with every different kind of food imaginable. They were standing by the first food booth, a pizza vendor with a large sign that said it was New York style. The slices were huge, each the size of two normal ones and they were thin crust with plenty of cheese and sauce.

"That pizza looks great to me, actually," Isabella said, her mouth watering as they opened an oven and the smell of freshly baked pizza wafted over her.

Aidan got slices for each of them with a couple of sodas and they carried their food over to the music area, where people were already sitting and waiting for the main band to start. They settled themselves on an empty bench and started eating.

The pizza was delicious and they both inhaled it. Isabella

was perfectly full but Aidan went to get another slice while she saved their seats.

She sat watching the crowd while waiting for Aidan to return and thought for a moment that she saw a glimpse of Travis. He got closer and she saw that it definitely was him and he was with someone who was wearing ridiculously high heels and had long, very blonde hair. What was he doing with Bethany, of all people? Travis looked up at that moment and noticed Isabella as well, and he and Bethany made their way over to her.

"Hi, Isabella," Bethany drawled as she linked her arm through Travis's. "Are you here all by yourself?" Her voice was sugary sweet and Isabella had to fight the urge to snap at her. "No, Aidan is getting more pizza. He'll be back in a minute." She glanced at Travis. "I didn't realize you were coming tonight."

"I wasn't planning on it," he admitted. "But when I stopped at the market to pick up a few things, I ran into Bethany and she was saying how she was dying to come but had no one to go with. So here we are."

"That was nice of you," Isabella said sweetly, for Bethany's benefit. Bethany just tossed her hair and looked bored.

"Let's go," she tugged on his arm to lead him away. "We haven't seen anything yet."

"All right. Enjoy the rest of your night," Travis said as Aidan returned and claimed his seat next to Isabella. They said a quick hello, and then Travis and Bethany were off.

"They looked good together," Aidan commented. "Have they been dating long?"

"No, this is their first date," Isabella said as the music started and they turned their attention to the stage. She didn't know why it bothered her, seeing the two of them together. Bethany just rubbed her the wrong way and she didn't think she would be good for Travis at all. But, she had to admit, they did look good together, such total opposites. Travis especially looked good that evening. He was out of his suit and dressed casually in jeans and a pale yellow button-down shirt that made his dark brown hair look black and his green eyes even more vivid. She glanced at Aidan and realized he was her complete opposite, too, with his pale blonde hair. It was hanging loose tonight, kept out of his face by a baseball cap that he wore backwards, which gave him more of an urban look, and of course it worked on him.

The band played for a little over an hour. The music was excellent and Isabella lost herself in each song until, each time the music ended, in the brief break in between songs, she glanced around, but never saw Travis and Bethany again. Bethany must not be into music.

They stopped to look at a few more booths as they walked out and shared a dessert, a fried dough that was perfect for sharing. It was the size of a dinner-plate and smothered in melted butter and dusted with both confectioner's sugar and cinnamon. Isabella tore off a small piece and it melted in her mouth, sugary goodness that she indulged in maybe once a year. Within minutes, they polished it off and then made their way to the car.

The drive home went by quickly as Aidan talked animatedly about the different artists he'd met and what he'd liked about them. It was just past ten when they pulled into the visitor spot by Isabella's condo. She was still full of energy and not ready for the night to end.

"Would you like to come in for a coffee?" she asked.

Aidan hesitated for just a second before saying, "Sure, why not?"

It only took a few minutes to make the coffee and while it was brewing, Aidan walked around the living room, taking in the wood sculpture in the corner that Isabella had inherited from her grandmother years ago. It was of two couples sharing an intimate and romantic kiss and Isabella had always loved it.

"You have some nice pieces here," Aidan said as Isabella handed him a steaming mug of coffee.

"Thank you. Do you need anything for the coffee? Cream or sugar?"

Aidan was already walking toward another painting on the wall. "No, I drink it black."

That was another thing they had in common. Isabella joined him by the painting.

"I actually got that one a few years ago at the Sweet Pea Festival. It's one of my favorites." It was a brightly colored abstract picture of a boat at a marina, and she had fallen in love with it instantly and had to have it. That was how she bought all of the artwork she'd collected over the years, when it gave her that kind of visceral reaction, drew her to it completely. That Aidan had the ability to create art like that was awe-inspiring.

"Do you paint at all?" Aidan asked and Isabella chuckled in response.

"No, I have zero talent for it. Jen and I went to a paint night last year at Delancey's. That's when twenty-five or so people gather at a restaurant, have cocktails and maybe a bite to eat and then everyone paints the same image. The class is led by the artist of the original painting and he talks everyone through it. Kind of like a paint by numbers. Though no two painting really looked the same at the end. It was really fun, actually."

"Do you have it here? Can I see it?"

"No, it's at my mother's. I was going to throw it out and she insisted on taking it. I think she put it in the guest room."

"I bet she said it was wonderful," Aidan said as he went to sip his coffee.

"That's what mothers do," Isabella agreed.

They chatted easily as they finished their coffee, and then Isabella couldn't hold back a yawn.

"I think that's my cue," Aidan said with a laugh as he set his mug in the sink.

"I'm sorry, that was rude."

"Not at all. Are you up for round two tomorrow night? There are twice as many bands and I'd love to see them with you."

"Sure, that sounds great." Isabella walked Aidan to the door and before he opened it, he wrapped his arms around her and gave her a quick, soft kiss. It was over in seconds. She told herself that the reason she felt nothing was because it was so fast.

"I'll see you tomorrow." He opened the door and as he walked to his car, Isabella glanced toward the end of the condo building, where Bethany's unit was. There was a car in her visitor spot also, a familiar large truck.

BETHANY WAS EASY ENOUGH TO SPEND TIME WITH. WHEN Travis had run into her at the grocery store, he'd still been in a down mood and was filling his basket with all kinds of junk, stuff he normally avoided like Oreos, chips and onion dip, frozen pizza and a six-pack of beer. His plan had been to just go home, have a cold beer, stuff his face and feel a bit sorry for himself. It seemed like a good enough plan.

But then he literally almost bumped into Bethany's cart on his mission to get to the Oreo double-stuffs. They'd gotten to talking and she seemed so sweet and a bit lost when she confessed that she was dying to go to the Sweet Pea Festival but didn't feel comfortable going by herself. He'd found himself offering to take her and abandoning his pity party plan. He still followed through with buying everything, though, as it would make it easier to have it all on hand for the next time he needed it.

He actually had a good time with Bethany at the festival. She was a chatterbox and talked non-stop, which was fine by him; all he had to do was nod every now and then. She was also very complimentary, telling him how handsome he looked when he came to pick her up. It was music to his ears to have that kind of attention and he soaked it up. Still, it was bittersweet running into Isabella and Aidan. He'd known it was likely inevitable if they were going to be there the same night. It was hard seeing the two of them together, though, and Isabella looked so happy.

But, it was also nice to be seen with someone like Bethany. She was a beautiful girl and turned many heads as they strolled through the festival. Isabella had looked surprised to see the two of them together. He got the sense that she wasn't a fan of Bethany, but that didn't concern him. He didn't care for Aidan, either. He was a nice enough guy, but Travis truly didn't think he was right for Isabella and it wasn't just because he wanted her for himself.

"Do you take anything in your coffee?"

Travis snapped back to attention. Bethany had invited him into her condo when he'd driven her home, and he'd been so annoyed when he pulled in to park and had seen Aidan's car in front of Isabella's condo that he'd been distracted ever since.

"Yes, please, extra sugar and cream if you have it."

"I have plenty of extra sugar, and I always have cream," Bethany purred as she added both to his mug and then slowly stirred. "Here you go." She handed him the mug and he took a small sip. She had added just the right amounts and it was delicious.

"Thank you."

"It's nothing. I really appreciate you taking me to the festival tonight. I was dying to go and had a great time." Bethany was looking at him with warmth and appreciation, and interest. Impulsively, he reacted to that by asking, "I know it's last minute, but do you have any plans tomorrow night? I'd love to take you to dinner."

"I did have plans, actually," Bethany drawled, "but they fell through earlier today, so I'm available and I'd love to go out with you."

"Great, it's a date, then." Travis finished his coffee and then gave Bethany a quick hug. "I'll come by around six tomorrow."

As he stepped outside, he was pleased to see that Isabella's visitor spot was now empty.

***

ISABELLA WOKE THE NEXT MORNING TO THE SOFT TAP OF A PAW across her cheek. She ignored it, and then a moment later the tap came again, but this time with a hint of claw. Jolene did not like to be ignored. Isabella sighed and reached for her cell phone which she kept on the night stand by her bed. It was ten past eight; no wonder Jolene was getting impatient. She was used to eating an hour earlier. Isabella rarely slept this late. She stretched and then eased herself out of bed, fed Jolene immediately. She made a cup of coffee and curled up on her sofa and wrapped herself in a fleece throw. By the time she was almost done with her coffee, she was beginning to feel more awake and got up to make a second cup. As it was brewing, her phone rang and she checked the caller ID. It was Anna.

"I know I told you to call me, but I have no life and

couldn't wait. How was the date?" Before Isabella could respond, she added anxiously, "He's not still there is he?"

Isabella chucked. "Hardly."

"It didn't go well?" Anna sounded disappointed.

"No, it went fine, but I'm not about to jump into bed with anyone that quickly, even Aidan. I was lucky I got a kiss."

"He kissed you? How was it?"

Isabella thought about that for a moment, "It was okay, fine. Just a quick good night kiss."

"Oh, that's it?"

"Yeah. That's okay, though. We had fun. We're going out tonight, too."

"You are? Well, that's good then. Back to the fair?"

"Yeah, we only saw about half of the artists and Aidan said the really good bands are playing tonight, some kind of bluesy rock music. Oh, and we saw Travis there, with Bethany."

"Southern Belle Bethany? High heels and fake fluffy blond Bethany?"

"The one and only."

"I thought Travis seemed smarter than that."

"He said they ran into each other and she suggested it."

"That, I can see."

"They seemed pretty into each other. His truck was at her condo when Aidan left."

"No kidding. Well, you just never know. I wouldn't have pegged her to be his type at all."

"I suspect that Bethany is most men's type. Pretty and blond is always a popular combo. Add in a Southern drawl and she could probably have her pick of guys around here."

"Fake Southern drawl. But I think you're probably right, and that's a depressing thought."

"I don't think she's right for him, but what do I know?"

Isabella said as she brought her fresh cup of coffee back to the sofa and pulled the throw over her again.

"So, back to you and Aidan. You're going out again tonight. That seems promising. He must have had a good time to see you again so soon."

"We did have fun, but I think it might be more that he really wants to go back to the festival." Isabella laughed.

"Well, maybe you'll get a proper kiss this time." Anna sounded hopeful.

"Maybe. I'll let you know tomorrow."

They chatted a few more minutes and then Anna had to run one of her boys to a friend's house. Jolene jumped up on the sofa, in a happy mood now that her belly was full. She curled up at Isabella's feet and purred loudly while she sipped the rest of her coffee. She didn't know why it had bothered her so much to see Travis with Bethany. She didn't like the way Bethany had been hanging on him, her arm linked with his and him looking so happy about it. Her gut just didn't like or trust Bethany. She considered Travis a good friend, especially as they'd been spending more time together recently, and she didn't want to see her hurt him. She flashed back to the pool when Travis had wrapped his arms around her to keep her from falling. How good it had felt and how she expected to have that feeling when Aidan kissed her. Hopefully, they might kiss again tonight and it would be amazing.

IT WASN'T AMAZING. THE NIGHT HAD BEEN FUN ENOUGH. THE bands were great and the food was delicious. Aidan had Indian this time and she went for the pizza again. They chatted easily enough, but Aidan brought Missy up several times, asking how she was doing and saying again how impressed he was with her and how he thought she was going to do so well as a realtor. It actually started to grate on her nerves a bit toward the end of the night when he mentioned her yet again. But still, he was more than willing to come inside again for coffee and when he finally kissed her while they were sitting comfortably on Isabella's sofa, it lasted a little longer than the night before and it was fine, but to say there were no fireworks would be an understatement.

Aidan jumped up after a few minutes, ran his hand through his hair and muttered something about having to get up early. Isabella walked him to the door and he was off, after saying that he'd had a great time and that they should do it again sometime. But, he didn't make any kind of a plan and Isabella shut the door behind him, feeling disappointed by the lack of a spark, and that he hadn't set a firm date for them to go out again.

CHAPTER 11

"**D**o you think a relationship is doomed if there's no physical chemistry at the beginning?" Isabella asked her sister. It was Monday night and they were gathered at their mother's house for the usual family dinner. Uncle Jim hadn't yet arrived and her mother and step-father had run to the store for a loaf of bread while she and Jen put a salad together.

"No sparks, you mean?" Jen clarified and Isabella nodded.

"That's a tough one. I suppose it's possible. It's never been my experience, though." She blushed a little and Isabella guessed she was thinking of Ian. The energy level when the two of them were near each other was a tangible thing.

"You were attracted to Ian immediately?"

"And how. We literally bumped into each other at that pub in Dublin and the minute his hand touched mine the electricity was off the charts." She made a face and then added, "I'm sorry, that's probably not what you wanted to hear."

"It was different for me and Helen," Uncle Jim said as he slowly walked into the room and sat on a stool next to Isabella. "We barely knew each other when we first started dating. All I knew was she was pretty and smelled real nice. But when we first kissed, it wasn't anything special. I broke up with her because of it, actually."

"You did?" Isabella was confused. They'd been married for over fifty years and Uncle Jim always referred to Aunt Helen as 'the love of my life.'

"Sure did. I took up with Angela Smith, and she started dating Charlie Hodges. The minute I saw her out with him, everything changed. I didn't like it one bit. I did everything I could to get her back and when she finally agreed to go out with me again and the next time I kissed her, it was completely different. I think it must have just been cold feet at first. If it wasn't for Charlie, I might have missed out on the love of my life."

They were all quiet for a moment and then Jen said, "I think things are different now, maybe."

"Maybe. Maybe not. People are people." Uncle Jim said as her mother and step-father walked in holding a large loaf of Italian bread. Her step-father sliced the bread and put it on the plate with a stick of butter while her mother took a tray of chicken cutlets that had been keeping warm in the oven and transferred them onto a platter and brought that to the table. Isabella grabbed the large bowl of pasta and tomato sauce, and Jen set the salad on the table and then they all sat down to eat.

"I saw that young man yesterday, the one you went kayaking with," Uncle Jim said as they were almost done eating.

"Travis?"

"He was with a real pretty girl. Long, blond hair, nice dress and highest heels I've seen in a long time."

"Where did you see them?" Isabella was curious.

"They were heading into the movies late yesterday afternoon. I was on my way into the pharmacy next door."

"Is he dating someone new?" Jen asked.

"It seems that way." She told them all about Bethany. "She's probably a nice person, but I don't think she's right for him."

"He looked pretty happy to me," Uncle Jim said as he went for his last bite of chicken.

"I actually thought the two of you would have made a good couple," Jen said. "I could swear he seemed interested."

"Well, I'm sure if he was, I never encouraged it. I never used to think of him that way."

Jen raised her eyebrow at that. "Are you feeling differently now?"

Isabella wasn't sure how she was feeling about anything. "I've never been interested before. I don't see how that would suddenly change. Besides, it would be too late anyway."

"It's never too late. Feelings can change." Uncle Jim said wisely, then added, "Pass the pasta, please?"

THE REST OF THE WEEK FLEW BY AND ISABELLA WAS GLAD WHEN Friday rolled around. When she and Anna took their usual coffee break around three, they chatted about Anna's upcoming party that night.

"What do you want me to bring?" Isabella asked.

"Just a bottle of wine, and keep it in the paper bag so we can put a number on it and hide the label."

"That's it? Are you sure? Do you need any food?"

Anna thought about that for a minute. "Well, your dip would be great, but I don't want to put you to any trouble."

"Don't be ridiculous, that dip takes like two minutes to make. It's the one thing I've perfected." Isabella smiled as she reached for her coffee.

"Thanks, that would be great. I think I'm good otherwise."

"How many people are you expecting?" Isabella asked.

"Maybe fifteen or twenty. You'll know most of them."

"Is Travis coming?"

"He said he was. Christian and Molly, too, and Dan and Traci. Have you heard from Aidan?"

"He called last night, said had to go to New York suddenly on business and that he'd be back sometime next week." He'd said he would call when he was back, but seemed a bit distant so Isabella wasn't sure what to think.

"Is Travis bringing Bethany?" She hoped not.

"I don't think so. He didn't mention it and I didn't suggest it. I did invite Missy but she said she's going to be out of town this weekend too and that she was sorry to miss it."

"I'm so glad you are doing this. It'll be fun." Anna used to throw the best parties and she was a wonderful cook. Isabella knew there would be no shortage of food.

"I told everyone to come around six thirty, but why don't you come a little earlier?"

"I'll plan on about a quarter to six, to help you get everything set up."

"Perfect!"

ISABELLA MADE THE DIP, COVERED THE BOWL IN PLASTIC WRAP and then went upstairs to change. She decided on a dressy white t-shirt, dark blue skinny jeans and her favorite red cowboy boots. Jolene was right behind her as she came down the stairs, reminding her that it was time for her to eat, too. She gave her a can of food and then was on her way to Anna's.

Anna's downstairs area was basically one big room. The kitchen flowed into the dining and living area and there were candles scattered everywhere, glowing merrily. The smells when she'd walked in the door were amazing. Isabella picked up the scent of melted cheese and mushrooms.

"You made your baked stuffed mushrooms?" she asked as she set the bowl of dip on the counter.

"I had to. I haven't made them in ages and they're so good." Anna's mushrooms were legendary. Isabella had no idea how she made them but knew there was all kinds of deliciousness inside: chopped proscuitto, blue cheese, buttery bread crumbs and who knew what else.

"Where do you want the wine?" Isabella was still holding her bottle in its brown paper bag.

"Why don't you set it over on that side table, by the window, and put the number one on it. There's a marker there so everyone can write the numbers down as they line them up." Isabella did that and then returned to the kitchen island where Anna was scooping fresh avocado into a bowl to make guacamole. Isabella was glad she'd had a light lunch.

"I figured this would go well with your dip. I also have lots of cheeses and crackers. Thought that would be good for wine tasting. There are chicken salad sandwiches and coffee cake for later, too."

Everyone loved Anna's chicken salad. It was the simplest of sandwiches but they always disappeared in minutes. Toward the end of the evening when people were starting to feel a bit hungry again, she would put out the sandwiches and the cake. That was the routine whenever Anna used to have people over for card night or parties.

By a quarter to seven, just about everyone was there except for Travis. He finally walked through the door ten minutes later, still in his suit. Anna walked over to greet him and he gave her a hug and an apology.

"I'm sorry I was running late. Had a client meeting that ran much longer than anticipated." He handed her a box of buffalo chicken wings that looked like they were from the takeout BBQ place near his office. Anna gratefully accepted them and directed him to bring his bottle of wine to the table with the others.

Isabella walked over to say hello and Travis gave her a hug and then looked a bit sheepish as he saw how casually everyone was dressed. "I came right from the office, but I suppose I could at least take the tie off?"

"And the jacket, too," she added with a smile. He pulled off the tie and shrugged out of his jacket. Anna, perfect hostess that she was, appeared to take his clothes and stash them out of the way.

"There's tons of food. Are you hungry?" Isabella asked.

"Starving. I was too busy for lunch—one of those days. You know how it is." He grinned and Isabella caught her breath. How had she never really noticed those deep green eyes and that he had dimples when he smiled big. Dimples.

"You should start with one of Anna's mushrooms, before they're gone."

"Sounds good, show me the way."

Isabella led him over to the kitchen island where Anna had everything set out, buffet style. She had made a few additional appetizers and others had brought things over too. Anna already had the wings Travis brought on a platter and Isabella reached for one. She'd been nibbling ever since she arrived and now decided to take a small plate and join Travis. They pulled stools up to the far side of the island and munched away while Anna called everyone to attention and explained how the wine tasting would work.

"There're pencils and sheets of paper on the counter, so everyone grab one of each so you can make note of which wines you like or hate." She smiled at that and then continued. "We'll start with number one and pour a bit for everyone, and then on to the next. Oh, there're a few buckets around too, in case you want to spit or dump any of the wine out. Don't feel like you have to drink it all. In a true wine tasting, you would spit it all out, but I can't imagine doing that," she admitted, and then added, "Oh, and the wine glasses are on the table with the wine, just grab one and we'll start in a minute."

"Do you need a glass?" Travis asked hesitantly as he knew Isabella rarely drank. "Yes, please. I'm going to try a little tonight." He smiled at that and returned a moment later with a glass for each of them.

"So, where's Aidan tonight?" he asked as he sat back down.

Isabella frowned and then said, "He's away on business."

"Trouble in paradise?" Travis raised his eyebrow as he reached for another mushroom.

"Not trouble, exactly. Just not sure about things," Isabella admitted, and then asked, "What about you? And Bethany?"

"What about her?" Travis asked.

"I thought you might bring her tonight."

"Anna invited me and didn't mention anything about Bethany or to bring anyone. Besides, it's not like we're serious. It's just been a few dates. She's a nice girl, though." He smiled at that and Isabella felt a sudden urge to kick him. Instead, she reached for another chicken wing and took a big bite.

Traci and Dan walked over then, followed soon after by Molly and Christian as the wine tasting got underway. Isabella chatted easily with everyone and noticed, not for the first time, how well Molly and Christian suited each other. People had asked her before if it bothered her to be around them, and she'd worried, at first, that it might, but was pleasantly surprised to find that she felt nothing but happiness for them. There was no lingering bitterness or sadness, which only confirmed that the relationship had never been more than superficial for either of them. She had enjoyed Christian's company, but she'd never felt crazy fireworks with him, either.

Travis accidentally brushed her hand as he reached for a piece of cheese and Isabella jumped at the contact.

"Sorry, didn't mean to startle you. I'm just after the cheese."

Isabella pushed the plate closer to him and rubbed her hand. Once again, just the touch of his hand had made her react so strongly. It didn't make sense. How could she have such a strong physical reaction to someone she'd never been drawn to romantically?

"Isabella, I've been meaning to thank you for sending Aidan my way," Traci said warmly.

"You sent him to Traci?" Travis asked.

"I helped him get his place ready to move into," Traci explained.

Travis was quiet for a minute and then said, "I might need your help soon, too."

Traci and Isabella exchanged glances, wondering what he was talking about.

"You want to decorate your condo?" Traci asked. Travis lived in a small condo a block away from his office. Isabella had never seen it, but he'd told her it was basically just a place to sleep—small, with a convenient location.

"I think it's time for me to move into a real house, and put the condo on the market." He looked at Isabella. "I thought maybe you could help me with that part and then once I find something, Traci can work her magic."

"Wow, that's a big step. What brought that on?" Traci seemed surprised and Isabella was, too. He'd never mentioned any interest in moving.

"It's something I've been thinking about for a while. Just feels like it might be the right time."

Isabella wondered if Bethany had anything to do with this decision and the thought irritated her.

"How are you liking the wine tasting?" Travis asked as she took a sip of wine number four.

"It's a fun idea and I like that it's small sips. I think after a while, it might be hard to tell them apart, though."

"Well, we have to take notes like Anna said, so we'll remember which ones we like." He had a teasing tone to his voice and it made Isabella smile.

"Okay, how would you describe this one, then?" she asked.

He thought about that for a minute, then took another small sip and swirled it around in his mouth before swallowing.

"Jammy. Full-bodied. Ripe and lush," he said intently as he looked right at her and Isabella suddenly felt a bit breathless. "What do you think?"

"Um, definitely fruity and smooth. I like it." She took another big sip.

"I love this one. Write it down. Number four is a winner." Travis winked at her and Isabella felt a blush coming on. What was happening to her?

They continued on like that through all seventeen wines. It was just a sip or two of each, but they added up to several glasses at least and since Isabella hadn't had a drop to drink in ages, it hit her harder than the rest of them. She wasn't drunk, but knew she had no business driving.

Anna put out the sandwiches and the coffee cake and everyone inhaled them. Within minutes, there was nothing left but crumbs. Isabella was suddenly feeling very full and sleepy.

"I can't wait to go to bed," she admitted to Travis.

He looked at her closely. "I'll drive you home."

"That's probably a good idea," she agreed.

People were starting to leave by then and Anna came by and noticed that Isabella could barely keep her eyes open.

"Do you want to stay here? You can sleep in one of the boys' rooms."

"I told her I'll give her a lift home," Travis said.

"Oh, okay, good. Thank you."

They made their way out to his truck and Isabella woke up a bit as the cooler air hit her face. The drive back to her condo was less than ten minutes and Travis opened her door for her and then walked her inside.

He went to give her a hug good-bye and Isabella impulsively kissed his cheek then brushed his lips and he immediately pulled back and then swore at the hurt in her eyes. "Aw, hell. I shouldn't be doing this."

He pulled her in tighter then and kissed her like he'd been wanting to kiss her for as long as he could remember.

CHAPTER 12

Isabella woke the next morning to a pounding head and a nervousness about a dream that seemed a bit too real. Had she really thrown herself at Travis and kissed him? And had he kissed her back in a way that made her body tingle from head to toe?

"Jolene, this is why I don't drink," she said to the small cat who was walking around her pillow and purring loudly.

She slowly eased herself out of bed and followed Jolene downstairs, fed her a can of food and then hovered by the coffee machine, willing it to make the coffee faster. As soon as it stopped brewing, she took the mug of hot coffee and went into the living room. She found her favorite chair, the one that overlooked the outside patio, pond, and mountains beyond, and settled herself comfortably with a soft throw blanket over her lap. Isabella liked to be warm and cozy and she knew that it was going to be a lazy kind of day. She didn't have to be anywhere, had the day completely off from all responsibilities and had no desire to leave her condo. A good book and maybe an old movie marathon seemed like a great idea.

She'd just gotten up to make a second cup of coffee when

her phone rang, and the caller ID said it was Travis. She felt a combination of nervousness and embarrassment as she answered, "Hello?"

"Good morning, sunshine," his voice rang out, full of energy.

"You're obviously feeling better this morning than I am," she said dryly.

"A tad under the weather? I am sorry to hear that. I just called to see if you want a ride over to Anna's to get your car? I am going to be heading your way shortly."

"Oh, okay, sure. That would be great, thanks." Isabella had completely forgotten that she'd left her car at Anna's. That settled any lingering doubt as to if she'd been dreaming. She had kissed Travis, quite thoroughly, and now he was on his way over.

"See you in about five," he said.

Isabella ran upstairs to get dressed. She wasn't up to making much effort, but still wanted to look somewhat decent. Her baby blue sweat suit and a white tank top underneath the hooded jacket would be perfect. She loved this sweat suit—the material was snuggly soft and it was actually flattering as far as sweat suits go—it hugged her curves ever so slightly. She ran a brush through her hair and as she came back downstairs, there was a tap on the door. She looked around the room for her purse, found it on the kitchen table, slung it over her shoulders and then answered the door. Travis was standing there, holding a small box of donut holes and two coffees.

"Figured you probably can't get enough of this stuff today, and that you haven't eaten yet?" he said with a smile. He looked all bright-eyed and bushy-tailed, freshly showered with still-damp hair and in a crisp white polo shirt and well-fitting, faded jeans.

"No, not a bite yet," Isabella confirmed. "Thanks for the coffee. It's just starting to wake me up now."

"You're ready to go?"

"All set."

They settled into Travis's truck and he flipped open the box of donuts and popped one in his mouth. Isabella selected a chocolate glazed one, and did the same. They were just a mile from the house when her phone rang again and it was Jen. That was odd. Her sister was not a morning person. Immediately, Isabella sensed that something was wrong as she answered the call.

"Hi, Jen. Is everything okay?"

"No." Her usually confident sister's voice was shaky. "It's Uncle Jim. His neighbor found him face down in his driveway, unresponsive, and called an ambulance. They don't know what happened, if he had a heart attack or just fell. The neighbor said his arm was black."

"Black? That doesn't sound good." The instant Jen told her something had happened to Uncle Jim, her eyes immediately began to water.

"I know. I'm on my way to the hospital. Mom and Bill are heading over, too. I'll see you there?"

"On my way now," Isabella said.

"What is it?" Travis asked, worry in his voice. Isabella couldn't speak for a moment. She had to calm herself or she'd burst into tears.

"It's Uncle Jim. They took him by ambulance to the hospital. No one knows what happened to him." It was too late; the tears were running down her face at this point.

Travis slowed the car and turned onto a side road.

"What are you doing?" They were only a few minutes from Anna's at this point.

"You're too upset to drive and I don't blame you. I'll take you there."

When they arrived at the hospital, Travis found a spot near the emergency entrance and they hurried inside. Jen and her mother and step-father were already sitting in the waiting room. They walked over to them and asked if there was any news.

"Nothing yet. They're running a bunch of tests. It may be a while. They're not sure how long Uncle Jim was lying there before the neighbor found him," Jen told them. Her mother wasn't saying a word and Isabella suspected she was trying to keep it together. They were all worried sick about Uncle Jim. He wasn't young and he was on a bunch of different heart meds after his first heart attack ten years ago.

"Thank you for driving me here," Isabella said to Travis.

"Of course," he said simply as he settled into a chair and took a sip of the coffee they'd brought in with them.

"Jen could probably bring me home. I don't want to keep you."

"You're not keeping me from anything. My day is wide open and I don't need to be anywhere."

"Okay."

The next two hours dragged on and felt like four as they waited to hear something, any kind of an update on Uncle Jim. All they knew was that he was in the ICU section of the ER and that they were still running tests. Travis made a run to the cafeteria for more coffee for everyone, and as soon as he walked away, Jen asked the question they were all curious about. "what is up with you and Travis this morning?"

Isabella fought to keep from blushing as she said, "Nothing, really. He was nice enough to give me a ride home last night after I had a little too much wine. He swung by this morning to give me a ride back to Anna's to get my car when you called and I immediately started crying when I tried to tell him what happened to Uncle Jim. He said I was too upset to drive, turned his truck around and brought me here."

"That's it?" Jen raised her eyebrows and Isabella knew she thought there was more to the story. Jen didn't miss much.

"That was very kind of him," their mother said as she dabbed at her own eyes. Her step-father squeezed her mother's hand and she smiled gratefully at him.

Travis returned with the coffees and about twenty minutes later, a very young-looking doctor came over to them.

"Are you the Graham family?" he asked, and when they all nodded, he went on to give them the update.

"We're still running a few more tests, but the good news is that your uncle should be fine. He's awake now and admitted that he'd stopped taking some of his heart medicines because he was feeling so good and didn't think he needed them anymore." They glanced at each other; that was so Uncle Jim.

"It looks like he may have fractured his hip, just a hairline fracture that should heal up quickly, but he'll need to be in rehab for a few weeks so they can keep an eye on him and work with him to make sure he's getting his meds and doing some physical therapy."

"What about his arm?" Jen asked. "The neighbor said it was black when he found him."

"Yes, that is due to two things. He was supposed to be monitoring his blood thinner levels on a weekly basis and stopped coming in to the center about a month ago. At the same time, he learned how to cook spinach and has been eating large amounts of it. That interfered with the blood thinner med. If he'd been coming, they would have caught that and adjusted the amount accordingly, but since he didn't, the result was a black arm. We've fixed that, and he's promised to let them know each week if he's eating unusual amounts of spinach." The doctor smiled at that and Isabella could almost feel their whole group relax. Uncle Jim was going to be okay.

"Can we go in and see him now?" their mother asked.

"Yes. Just two at a time, though, and family only."

Their mother and step-father went in first, and about twenty minutes later came back to let Jen and Isabella go in.

Isabella turned to Travis then. "Thank you so much for staying, but I think we're probably going to be here for a while. Jen can give me a ride back."

"Okay," Travis agreed, and added, "I'm glad he's all right."

"Young man, I just want to thank you as well for giving Isabella a ride home last night and for bringing her here this morning. I'm very grateful. "Her mother's voice was still a bit wobbly with emotion.

"It was nothing," Travis assured her. Then he turned to Isabella. "I'll call you later."

UNCLE JIM LOOKED SO SMALL IN HIS HOSPITAL BED. THE SKIN on his face appeared more delicate than usual, almost translucent and fragile, and the left side of his cheek was bruised and scraped from falling against the pavement.

"You came to see me!" His face lit up as Jen and Isabella walked in. Though his voice sounded weak, he was smiling and seemed in good spirits.

"We were so worried about you," Isabella said as she leaned over to kiss his cheek. Jen did the same, and then added, "How are you feeling?"

"A little banged up, but I'll be okay. They say I have to stay in that rehab for a few weeks. You know, I am not happy about that." They did know. Uncle Jim had stayed at a rehab after he had his heart attack years ago and had hated it. He was a homebody and liked being in his own bed, not surrounded by chirping monitors and people coming and going at all hours to check blood pressure and other stats.

"It won't be for long. You'll bounce back and be home before you know it, and of course we'll come bother you all the time," Isabella assured him.

"So what was up with the spinach, Uncle Jim?" Jen teased him.

"Your mother had me over for dinner a few weeks ago and showed me how to make it. I remembered that I used to love spinach. When Helen and I were first married, we were so poor that there was many a night when I had a spinach sandwich for supper." Isabella made a face at the thought of that.

"I love spinach sandwiches. You should really try one." Uncle Jim smiled and then added a bit contritely, "I guess maybe I overdid it."

"Uncle Jim, the doctor told us you'd stopped taking your meds. You know how important it is that you take them regularly, right?" Jen pulled his blanket up a bit when he shivered as the air conditioning kicked in with a cold blast.

"I didn't think I needed them anymore. I've been feeling great."

"It's partly because of the meds. We don't want this to happen again," Isabella said gently.

"I know. I told that doctor I'd take whatever medicine he wants me to take. I was just feeling so good, you know?" He looked sad and suddenly old and it broke Isabella's heart. She couldn't imagine a world without Uncle Jim in it. She took hold of his hand and squeezed it tenderly.

"You amaze and inspire me all the time. I know you'll be

feeling fine before you know it and flirting like mad with the nurses at that rehab."

"They do have pretty nurses there, from what I remember." A bit of a twinkle was back in his eyes again.

Jen and Isabella stayed for another half-hour until they could see Uncle Jim's eyes growing heavy, and then they carefully hugged him good-bye and promised to stop by later that day and then as often as they could in the days after that.

CHAPTER 13

Jen dropped Isabella off at Anna's house so she could pick up her car. Isabella was hoping that Anna would be there, so they could chat over a cup of coffee, but the only car in the driveway was her own when they arrived. So, Isabella drove home and then, after visiting Uncle Jim again later that afternoon, she was in for the evening and already in her pajamas heating up a bowl of soup when her phone rang and it was Travis.

"Hey, Isabella. Just checking in to see how the rest of your day went and how your uncle is doing?"

She filled him in and said he would be transferred to a rehab in the next few days once they made certain that no infections had set in.

"How was your day? Did you do anything productive?" she teased.

Travis chuckled. "I suppose so, if you count a few loads of laundry and a quick trip to the grocery store. Not very exciting."

"I should have done those things today, too, but I'm too tired to worry about it."

"You were busy with Uncle Jim. That's a good excuse." She could picture the smile on his face.

"Do you have a busy week ahead of you?" He was always busy, so she was sure he probably did, but it was nice to chat easily with him.

"Crazy, as usual. But, the end of the week looks a bit lighter. I was wondering if you might have some time Friday afternoon to ride around with me, look at some neighborhoods I like and start keeping an eye out for a house?"

"Sure." He seemed pretty serious about this, which surprised her a bit. She hadn't realized it was something he was thinking about moving on now.

"Great. How does two thirty work for you? I could swing by the office and we could head out from there?"

Isabella quickly checked her planner to see if she had anything booked yet for Friday afternoon and it was clear.

"That's perfect. I'll keep the rest of the afternoon open."

Before she knew it, Friday afternoon had rolled around and Travis was due to stop by the office any minute. Uncle Jim was settled into the rehab center and Isabella had stopped in every day, either at lunch or right after work, to visit with him. Today, she'd popped in around lunch time. He was in good spirits and already knew the names and life stories of all the nurses. Isabella hadn't heard a word from Aidan since he'd returned from New York, and was actually relieved. He must have come to the same conclusion that she had, that there was no real romantic spark between them.

She took a final sip of a coffee that had long since grown cold. As much as she loved coffee, she didn't drink nearly as much as it seemed because she often let it sit and get cold when she was distracted by a ringing phone or email that needed immediate attention.

"The Millers want to close in six weeks. Will that work for your sellers?" Isabella looked up to see Missy standing by her desk, cell phone in hand, waiting to get back to her buyers.

"I think so, let me check." Isabella put a quick call into her sellers, who answered on the first ring and were fine with the suggested closing date. Missy wandered off to call her buyers back with the good news. Isabella thought for a minute about how things were going with Missy. She'd had some concern a week or so ago when Missy received another referral from a mutual acquaintance that probably would have gone to Isabella if not for Missy, but then a similar situation went her way a week later. Missy was also very actively prospecting for new buyers, and as the realtor with the most listings in the office, Isabella had benefited from that more than once already. So, it looked as though she might lose the occasional client to Missy but in the long run, they might both make each other more money.

She did notice, though, that Missy wasn't her usual, perky self since she'd returned from her sudden out-of-town trip. She hadn't shared any details about it and had been very heads down and focused on her work since returning to the office on Tuesday. Isabella wondered if she and Jeremy were going through a rough patch or something, but Missy was very private about her social life. Isabella didn't give it another thought and turned her attention back to her email.

A few minutes later, she heard the front door open and then recognized Travis's voice talking to Anna, who was covering for Francie, their front desk receptionist who was out running an errand at the post office. Isabella stood up to walk out when her phone buzzed and she saw it was Anna. She picked it up quickly and said, "I'm on my way."

Travis smiled at her as she approached the front desk. He was wearing a dark, charcoal gray suit and a pale green dress shirt with a teal necktie. He looked relaxed and handsome, and Isabella felt a hint of butterflies in her stomach.

"You look nice," Travis said.

"Thank you. Are you ready to go?" Isabella appreciated the compliment. She was wearing one of her favorite work outfits, a slim-fitting pencil skirt in a deep navy blue with a soft, ivory colored silk top and a pair of low, pretty heels.

"Happy hunting!" Anna called after them as they walked out the door.

"Do you mind if I drive?" Travis asked when they stepped outside. Usually, Isabella drove clients to the houses or neighborhoods they wanted to look at.

"No, of course not," she said and followed him to his truck.

Once they were buckled in and heading out of the lot, Travis explained, "I thought it might be easier for me to drive because I can show you exactly which areas I like and drive by houses that look like the type of style I want.

"That makes sense." Isabella slipped into realtor mode and pulled out a small notepad and pen. "So, what exactly are you looking for? What are the must haves for the house itself?" She was ready to take notes.

"I'm thinking at least three or four bedrooms and an acre of land. A finished basement would be nice, with room for a pool table and a sofa or two so it can be a good place to watch the games or relax and play a little pool."

"I didn't realize you were that into pool."

"I love it, but don't play very often. Not that many places have tables around here. Do you play at all?"

"I haven't played in years, but I love it, too," Isabella confessed. She'd played often in college and had learned how from some of the customers that she served at a local pub near campus. The bar was packed with college students every night, but during the day it was mostly locals who came in the afternoon after working the six to two shift at a factory in town. Isabella had worked a few shifts tending bar in the afternoons and it was never very busy then, so in between refilling draft beers, they often invited her to play a few rounds and she was an eager student.

"We should play sometime," Travis said casually as he turned onto a road that led into one of Isabella's favorite neighborhoods. It was an older part of town, with bigger houses on at least an acre of land. The road was a windy one that kept climbing higher and higher until finally leveling off. When they came around a corner, the views over the rest of the town were breathtaking.

"This is a gorgeous area," Isabella commented as Travis slowed the truck down to take in the view.

"I've been keeping an eye on it for a while. I haven't seen any listings in this part of town, though, but maybe there's something I've missed?" His tone was hopeful and Isabella regretted what she had to share.

"Nothing has come on the market here in months, but it doesn't mean something won't come available. There are things we can do, too, to shake some listings loose."

Travis looked intrigued by that. "Like what?"

"We can contact everyone in the neighborhood and ask them if they've considered putting their home on the market, or if they know of any neighbors who might be thinking about it because we have an interested buyer."

"Does that really work?"

"Sometimes. It's all timing, really. If someone has been thinking about selling and then hears from us that we have a potentially interested buyer, it can tip them off the fence to at least see what the market has to offer."

"I suppose it's worth a shot." Travis seemed doubtful about the idea.

"You never know until you try," Isabella agreed, then added, "Why don't you point out the house styles that you like the most, and I can keep an eye out for similar ones in other areas, too—if you're open to other neighborhoods?"

"I am. This neighborhood is just my first choice, but there are other nice areas, too. I'll take you to my runner-up sections now."

They drove around for the next hour-and-a-half, looking at different areas and houses. The other areas did have some active listings, so Isabella pointed those houses out to Travis and he agreed to go see a few of them.

"Even if you don't decide to buy any of them, it will still be helpful to see what you like and don't like once we get inside them."

As they pulled back into Isabella's office parking lot, Travis debated whether or not to ask the question, but he couldn't stop himself. "I don't suppose you're free tonight?"

"For what?"

"Dinner at Delancey's, if you're up for it. Least I can do to thank you for riding around with me all afternoon."

She laughed at that, and then said, "well, it is my job."

"True, but still, you have to eat. Unless you already have a hot date?" He held his breath, hoping that wasn't the case.

"No, nothing planned and I am kind of hungry."

"Great. I need to run by the office then home to change. I'll be by in about a half-hour."

CHAPTER 14

Jolene came running when Isabella opened the door to her condo. She scooped up the little fur ball and gave her a hug.

"Hello, my love, how was your day?" she asked the cat who responded by starting to purr and rub against Isabella's cheek. She held her for a few more seconds until Jolene indicated that she'd had enough and Isabella set her down. Jolene immediately went to the kitchen cabinet where her food was kept and paced back and forth, waiting for Isabella to take the hint.

"Here you go." She set down a dish with her food and then went upstairs to get changed. She had about twenty minutes before Travis would be over. As much as she loved her outfit, if he was changing out of his suit, she'd be overdressed if she didn't do the same. She decided on jeans, a pale lilac top that had a boat neck and three-quarter length sleeves, and a pair of comfy leather sandals.

She had worried that there might be some awkwardness about the tipsy kiss after Anna's party, but it was as though it had never happened. She really wasn't sure what to think about Travis. As much as she'd enjoyed that kiss, she did wonder if it would have been the same if she hadn't been drinking. Maybe it wasn't really that wonderful? She was still concerned that she'd never thought of Travis romantically before and questioned whether it would be a good idea to start something. Or if he even wanted to?

What if the physical attraction were to fade? Would there be anything left? If she was going to be interested in him romantically, wouldn't it have already happened by now? That was the question that she kept coming back to and it made her hesitant to explore these new feelings. She also questioned whether it would be wise to date someone that she worked with. Helping him find a house was one thing, but they also regularly worked together on deals and sent business each other's way—was she willing to risk jeopardizing that if things didn't work out? It was a lot to consider. She was still deep in thought and brushing her teeth as she heard a knock on the door.

She opened the door to let him in and he gave her a quick hello hug which took her breath away. Not only did he look great in his deep navy blue cotton button-down shirt and tan khakis, he smelled amazing, too. How had she never noticed that before?

"You're okay with Delancey's still?" he asked as she looked around for her purse and found it on the kitchen table.

"Of course. It's my favorite restaurant in Beauville." It was also the best of the limited options available in town.

Travis drove and when they arrived at Delancey's, it was already packed, but they managed to get one of the last available tables.

"Five minutes later and we would have been on the waiting list." Travis said as the hostess led them to a table for two and handed them menus.

A few minutes later, a waitress appeared to take their drink order. Isabella ordered a soda water with lemon and Travis got a coke.

"No wine tonight?" he teased as the waitress walked away.

Isabella chuckled. "That was fun, but I prefer my soda water and lemon. You could have gotten something, though. Please don't not drink on my account." She knew he usually had a beer or glass of wine when he went out.

"I'm not much of a drinker really, either. Was more in the mood for a coke. Goes just as well with a good steak."

"I think that's what I'm having, too. I don't eat a lot of red meat, but it's so good here."

The waitress returned with their drinks and then took their orders, which were identical: two filets, cooked medium, baked potato and asparagus. When she walked away, Travis picked up his soda and said, "Cheers!"

Isabella lifted her glass and tapped it against his. "What are we toasting to?"

"Anything, everything, surviving another week, new beginnings..." She wasn't entirely sure what he meant by that and he must have read the confusion on her face because he continued on. "To finding me my dream house...and to a great evening."

"I think you've covered just about everything," she teased.

"I aim to please." He smiled at her then and held her glance for a moment. Isabella felt the butterflies return and the energy around them crackle. It was really the strangest thing. She tried to calm her emotions; she wasn't used to feeling out of control like this.

"How's Traci and Dan? Are they settling into married life?" She shifted the conversation away from them and relaxed a little. The waitress also returned with their salads then, and a basket of hot rolls. As they started eating, Travis answered her question.

"They're great. I've never seen my sister so happy. Dan seems to be adjusting just fine to having his business here, too. I don't think he's missed a beat."

"What does he do again?" She knew it was something to do with the stock market.

"He's an analyst and a trader. He trades his own account and analyzes the market and reports on both to his newsletter subscribers. His thing is options."

That's right, now it came back to her. Dan had gone to college in Chicago and stayed on after graduating, covering the options market for local financial publications.

"I wonder if he misses Chicago?" Isabella had never been there. Hadn't done much traveling at all, actually.

"He doesn't seem to. His life and family are here. I'm sure Chicago has lost its appeal."

"Did you ever want to live anywhere else?" she asked.

"In Montana? Or generally?"

"Both."

He thought about that for a moment. "For about five seconds, I thought it might be fun to live in New York City. It was a blast going to school there. But it's such a big city, so different from here. And crazy expensive. I don't know how kids even afford apartments there after graduating, unless they have trust funds or something."

"I've never been to New York. I'd love to go sometime."

"You should, though maybe you'll fall in love with the city and never want to come back. That happens, too."

"I doubt it. I love living here. Beauville is a great town."

"It really is," Travis agreed. "It's why I decided not to go to Bozeman, either. I never wanted to be in a big firm, on the partner track. I got a taste of it one summer and that was enough. The following summer, I worked with Evan Foley in the office I'm in now and he was close to retiring then. The agreement was that I'd come on with him for a few years and then when he was comfortable with how I was doing things and ready to retire, he could leave his business in good hands."

"Do you ever go back to New York to visit?"

"I've been back a few times, for weddings mostly, people I went to school with. It's been at least five years since I last went. No one hasn't gotten married lately," he said with a grin.

The waitress appeared then with their meals, and took their salad plates away. The steaks and asparagus were both blanketed with creamy bearnaise sauce and when Isabella cut into her steak, it was perfectly pink and delicious.

They continued to chat as they enjoyed their dinners and just as they were almost done and Isabella was thinking it had been such a perfect night so far, she caught a glimpse of a familiar head of fluffy blonde hair. Bethany and Missy were being seated by the hostess and were coming directly toward their table.

Missy stopped to say hello and Bethany glared at both of them before addressing Travis. "Nice to see both of you. Travis, I thought you'd mentioned that you had a work thing tonight?" Her voice was sugary sweet but the undertone was unmistakably cold.

"Isabella is helping me find a house. We were out all afternoon looking at places."

"I see." Then as it registered what he'd said, she warmed up and added, "I didn't realize you were going to buy a house. That is exciting. Don't forget we're still on for tomorrow night."

Travis looked decidedly uncomfortable at the reminder. "That's right. I'll see you then."

"Can't wait," she said in a flirty tone as she and Missy walked to their table.

"I didn't realize you were still dating Bethany," Isabella said quietly. Good thing she'd already finished most of her meal because her appetite was gone now. How stupid she was to think Travis was actually interested. Theirs was just a business relationship, always had been, and it looked like that's the way it would stay.

"We've just gone out on a few dates. I forgot that I'd promised her that we'd go to some fund-raising thing in Bozeman."

"Well, I'm sure that will be fun," she said stiffly as the waitress appeared to clear the table.

"I'm not looking forward to it," he assured her, but Isabella had her walls back up and just wanted to go home.

"Do you want to share a dessert?" he asked with a smile, trying to get things back to the way they were before Bethany showed up.

"I have no interest in dessert, sorry."

"Coffee?" He tried again.

"I'm all set, but if you want anything, feel free." When the waitress came back, Travis just asked for the check, paid it and then they left.

They were both quiet on the ride home, the happy mood from earlier replaced with an uncomfortable tenseness as Travis tried to engage Isabella in conversation that went nowhere. He pulled into her condo parking lot, parked, and then walked her to the door.

"Thank you for dinner. That was really nice of you," she said politely. But she didn't invite him in.

"I had a great night with you," he said softly.

"Good night, Travis." She reached to give him a quick hug good night before ducking in the door. But this time, he was the one to pull her in tight and surprised her with a kiss directly on the mouth. It was soft at first, but when she didn't resist, he deepened it and she gave in, surrendering to the same intense chemistry that she felt the first time. Only this time, completely sober, it was even stronger. She almost changed her mind about inviting him in, but then an image of Bethany invaded her thoughts and she remembered that he was going out with her tomorrow night. She pulled back and reached for the door.

"Have fun on your date tomorrow night."

CHAPTER 15

W hy the long face?" Uncle Jim asked the next day when Isabella stopped by the rehab to see him after her morning shift at the food pantry. She'd been smiling when she walked through the door and gave him a big hug and kiss, but after she'd been sitting for a few minutes, her thoughts had turned to Travis's date that evening with Bethany. She realized that she was actually jealous.

"It's nothing," she said lightly and smiled at Uncle Jim. He looked great; the color was back in his cheeks and the bulletin board by his bed was covered with get-well cards, mostly from women. Uncle Jim was a huge flirt, but it was totally innocent. He flirted with every woman he came across, from age twenty to his own, and his happy mood was infectious. People loved to be around him. Isabella was so relieved that he was feeling better and making good progress. He'd be able to go home in less than a month if he continued to improve.

"Boy trouble, I bet," he said wisely.

"Something like that," Isabella admitted.

"Which one is it? That blond artist? Or your lawyer friend?"

Isabella frowned, thinking of Travis, but instead just said, "I'm not dating Aidan, the artist, any more. There wasn't any real chemistry there."

"Chemistry is important. Did you give him that second chance I mentioned? Like with me and Helen?"

"No, I haven't heard from him. I'm pretty sure he felt the same way."

"Okay, then, maybe so. Maybe not, though. Promise me if you do hear from him that you'll at least go out with him one more time?" Uncle Jim seemed so adamant about this that Isabella couldn't help but agree. Especially as she didn't think it was likely that she would hear from Aidan now. As far as she knew, he he'd gotten back from New York a week ago.

"Sure. If I hear from him, I will." She reached over and gave one of Uncle Jim's hands a gentle squeeze and he smiled back at her.

"Good, now what about that other one? The lawyer? I heard you've been seeing him a little, and that he was the one who first brought you to see me in the hospital. He gets points for that, you know."

Isabella couldn't help but smile at that. Uncle Jim was just too cute.

"I think we're just friends. He has a date with someone else tonight. Bethany is new here, just moved to town a few weeks ago. She's slim, beautiful and very blonde."

"Hmmm. And you don't like her very much, do you?"

"I don't think you'd like her, either. She's a fake Southern Belle. Puts on that sugary sweet accent and bats her eyes for every guy she meets and must spend at least an hour on her hair in the morning. And she wears heels, everywhere. Who does that?"

Uncle Jim chuckled. "And you really don't like that she's going out with Travis tonight, do you?"

"No. I hate it," Isabella admitted. "He says that it means nothing, that she invited him to this thing they are going to over a week ago and he forgot all about it. She reminded him, though, when she saw us out to dinner at Delancey's."

Uncle Jim shifted himself up a bit straighter in his bed, and she could tell that he was fascinated by her story. He always liked to be up on all the gossip, so she knew he loved this kind of drama. She filled him in on the rest—how they'd been having such a great night, and had been out looking at houses earlier in the afternoon, and then Bethany bounced into the picture and completely burst her bubble. She didn't tell him about the good-night kiss, though. But he was quiet when she finished talking and looked as though he was debating asking her something. Finally, he spit it out.

"Did he kiss you good-night?"

"Uncle Jim!" Isabella was surprised that he asked.

"What? It's an important question. A key bit of necessary data."

Isabella chuckled at that. "Okay, yes, he did kiss me good-night."

Uncle Jim's eyes narrowed. She wasn't giving him enough information.

"A real kiss, or just a peck on the cheek?" That made her blush and he had his answer.

"Okay, then, a real kiss is something to consider. I'd say it keeps him in the game. You need to just relax and follow your gut with these two guys. Go with your gut. It won't steer you wrong."

———

"I THINK IT'S SO GREAT THAT YOU'RE BUYING A HOUSE IN ONE of the best neighborhoods in Beauville. Missy said that area is mostly two-acre lots. You'll have room to grow a family someday."

"Someday, maybe," Travis agreed as he took another sip of beer and then checked his watch. Would this night never end? It was still so early.

"I'm so glad we came to this, aren't you?" Bethany drawled as she tossed her hair and looked around the room.

"Sure, it's a good cause." The event they were attending was in Bozeman and was to benefit the local homeless shelters. It was held in the ballroom of the largest hotel in the city and nearly five hundred people were there. There were rumors that the governor might stop by. Bethany had informed him earlier that it was a really 'posh' event and a great chance for her to get to know the 'right' people. Travis had hated it from the moment he walked in. Not even the food was good; it was all foo-foo stuff that he had no interest in.

"I like to give back. It's so important, don't you think?" Bethany tossed her hair again and Travis couldn't help but wonder how sincere she was. He decided to find out.

"You know, Isabella helps manage the food pantry in Beauville. I know they are always looking for additional volunteers to help with deliveries, unloading and stocking the shelves and giving out food to the clients who come in. I'm sure she could add you to the schedule if you'd like to help?"

Bethany immediately made a face. "No, thanks, that doesn't sound like a good fit for me. How embarrassing for those people. It would be too hard for me to be so close to them."

Travis immediately took a step back in disgust. "Why? Poverty isn't contagious."

Bethany slapped his arm and laughed. "You're so funny! No, this is my kind of charity work, buying tickets to fun parties and helping to support the charities that way."

"Well, you're very good at it," he said dryly as he finished his beer and decided he definitely needed another. "Can I get you something?"

"Thank you. I'd love one."

The line for drinks was a long one, but Travis didn't mind waiting. It gave him a break from Bethany's mindless chatter. When he'd first met her, he hadn't minded in the least, and actually thought it was cute, that she was cute. She was a gorgeous girl, but the more he got to know her, the less attractive she seemed. Especially the way she'd ruined his night with Isabella, although that wasn't entirely her fault. He had agreed to go to this event with her. He had to find a way to make it up to Isabella, to show her how he really felt, and to make it clear to her that there really was nothing to worry about with Bethany. They wouldn't be going out again.

"I saw Travis this morning at the Muffin," Anna said as Isabella brought her coffee into the conference room to chat for a minute. They only had a few minutes as the rest of the office would be in early for the Monday meeting. When Isabella said nothing in response to that, Anna added, "He told me to tell you hello and that he'll be calling you this morning."

"Great, thanks." Isabella took a sip of her coffee and then changed the subject, asking how Anna's weekend had been. She and her boys had gone away camping with a neighbor and their kids.

"The kids had a blast. We survived. You know how I feel about camping." She made a face. "But I'd promised the boys we would go, so we did. Now, tell me what is going on with Travis?"

Isabella sighed and then filled her in.

"So he fell for her nonsense when he first met her. That doesn't mean anything. She's totally not his type. And from what you said, it sounds like this was something he agreed to before the two of you even kissed the first time."

"I think that is true."

"So, water under the bridge."

"I suppose."

"Don't be ridiculous. You have nothing to worry about with her."

THE REST OF THE DAY FLEW BY. TRAVIS HAD CALLED SOON after the morning meeting to say hello and see if Isabella was still going to try and arrange a few showings later that day or the next. She confirmed that she had been able to line up two for late afternoon, so he said he would stop by around four. Isabella spent most of the day in the office, working on different projects. One of them was the marketing campaign she'd mentioned to Travis. She put a letter together that would go out to every house in his first choice area, where there were no houses currently for sale, to see if they could encourage a new listing by letting the homeowners know they had a serious buyer that was interested in their neighborhood.

Missy was out of the office most of the day, but was back now and working quietly at her desk. Her phone rang, and after just a few minutes, she slammed it down and muttered something unintelligible. Mild-mannered Missy then took the bouquet of glorious red roses that had arrived that morning and slammed them in the trash can beside her desk.

"Fight with Jeremy?" Isabella said gently, wanting to help somehow. Missy looked up in surprise, her eyes wet and her mascara smudged.

"Yeah, something like that," she said as she grabbed a tissue and then ran off to the ladies' room. When she returned a few minutes later, there was no trace of any tears and she'd reapplied a cheerful shade of red lipstick. She didn't sit back down at her desk, though, just glanced at the clock which read almost four, grabbed her purse and said she had to go meet a client.

Travis arrived about ten minutes later, just after Isabella handed over the mailing project to Francie to finish. She would stuff all the envelopes with the signed letters and then run them to the post office.

"You look beautiful," Travis said as Isabella walked over to greet him. She had to admit, it was nice to hear.

"Thank you. Are you ready to go?" Isabella drove this time. The first house they were going to see was just a few miles from Travis's favorite area and still a very pretty part of town. The lot was just over an acre and the house had four bedrooms and three baths. It was a lot of house for one person.

"I know it seems like a big size for just me," Travis started to explain, almost as if he'd read her mind as they walked toward the front door. "But eventually I hope to fill up some of these other rooms. I just don't want to have to move again."

Isabella punched the key code into the lockbox that hung from the front door, removed the key and then let them in.

It was a beautiful house and relatively new, just five years old. Isabella explained that the husband was a sales executive for a large national corporation and had the home custom built for his family. They'd lived there for just a year when he took a new job and they had to relocate back East.

The house had all the features that Travis was looking for, including an already finished basement with a pool table that the owners were willing to include in the price of the house.

"I'm not surprised they want to leave this behind. They are a pain to move," Travis said as he ran his hands along the table's polished wood. "This one is a beauty, though." It was made of a gleaming mahogany wood and the felt top was a deep gray, which matched the blue-gray walls.

The kitchen was a winner with Travis, too. It was a cook's kitchen, with honed marble countertops, a double-oven and a six-burner gas stove set in the middle of the island, which faced floor-to-ceiling windows looking out over a valley and the mountains beyond.

"Do you like to cook?" she asked, and realized how much she didn't know about Travis.

"I love to play around in the kitchen, and I'm not half-bad. I don't do much cooking these days, though, as I live alone and my condo just has a small galley kitchen. A good kitchen is important to me."

"How do you like this one?"

He grinned. "This would be very fun to play in!"

They went upstairs and all the bedrooms were large with plenty of windows and light coming through.

"What do you think?" Travis asked as they entered the master bedroom and saw the attached large bathroom and walk-in closet.

"I'd kill for a closet like that," Isabella admitted. "The rest of the house isn't bad, either." She smiled as that was an under-statement. It was a lovely house.

"Yeah. It hits everything I'm looking for, except that neigh-borhood. But this one isn't bad at all."

"Are you ready to check out the other house?"

"Sure thing. Lead the way."

Isabella was careful to lock the door as they left and return the key to the lockbox. She then drove them to the next house which was just a few miles away and a little higher up on the hill and had a slightly nicer view. The house was similar in size and style, but didn't have a finished basement. Travis would have to do that if he decided on that house.

As they drove back to the office, Isabella debriefed him on the two houses. "So what did you think about them? What did you like?"

"I liked the first house the best, but loved the view of the second one. The second one had a decent kitchen, too, but I'd have to finish the basement. That's not too big of a deal, though. The pool table in the first one is pretty sweet."

"At least I have a good idea of what you like now."

"I'd say you pretty much nailed it." Out of the corner of her eye she could see Travis smiling.

"We sent a mailing off today, to the neighborhood you like. It will probably take a few days or maybe even longer, but we might get some interest. You never know."

"Well, I'm in no rush. I can wait and maybe look at any others that you think I should see."

"I can set you up on an email that will send you all the new listings in town if you want to see what is coming on the market, too. Some people like to have a feel for everything that is in their range out there."

"Sure, set it up. That would be interesting to keep an eye on."

Isabella pulled into the office parking lot, which was deserted by now as it was almost six.

"Okay, I'll keep you posted," Isabella said and waited for Travis to get out of the car. He didn't make any motion to move though.

"Are you having dinner with your family tonight?" he asked. She'd mentioned over the years how they often gathered early in the week for dinner, usually on Monday nights.

"No, Jen has something tonight so we're actually meeting up tomorrow instead."

"Oh, good. Why don't you come to my place for dinner, then? It's on your way home and I'm making one of my favorite recipes. Even though I have a good appetite, I can't eat it all."

Isabella hesitated, and Travis added, "Nothing fancy, I just thought it would be nice for us to hang out and you can see why I need to move." He chuckled at that and Isabella did, too.

"Okay, I'll follow you."

Travis's condo was just a few minutes down the road, a block away from his office, which meant he could walk to work.

"That's the best feature of this place—you can't beat the commute," he said as Isabella got out of her car and then walked over to his building. His unit was on the second floor and as he let them in, Isabella could see that it was a basic apartment style unit, all on one level with one bedroom, one bathroom, a fairly large living and dining area and a tiny kitchen.

"Welcome to my humble abode." Travis shrugged off his suit jacket and loosened his tie.

"It's a great place." Isabella admired the way it was decorated, which was with sleek black leather sofas, a steel and glass coffee table, stormy gray walls, black framed prints on the walls and an oversized TV. It was obvious a man lived here.

"Have a seat, make yourself comfortable." Travis indicated the two chairs at a small breakfast bar that separated the kitchen from the living area. She settled into one of them and could watch Travis as he cooked.

"Can I help you with anything?"

"No, thanks. I'm all set. This won't take long. Plus, there's really no room for anyone else in this kitchen, anyway." He flashed her a grin then, making his dimples dance and her heartbeat race a little.

"Can I get you anything to drink? I have some seltzer water and plenty of lemon or beer."

"Seltzer and lemon would be great, thanks."

Travis grabbed a lemon from a bag on the counter, sliced off a wedge and added it to the glass of seltzer water and ice that he'd just poured.

"So, what are you whipping up for us?" Isabella was impressed that he was going to cook for her.

"I probably should have asked this earlier, but do you like shrimp?" He looked worried suddenly, which made him all that much cuter to her.

"I love shrimp. All seafood actually."

"Oh, good. They had a sale at the market yesterday and the shrimp looked really good so I picked up a bag." He got the bag out of the freezer and set it on the counter, and Isabella could see that they were huge. He poured half the bag into a bowl and then set it in the sink and ran water over it.

"If I do that for a few minutes, it will thaw them out enough to saute them."

"How did you learn that?" Isabella had never seen anyone do that before.

"I worked in restaurant kitchens during my college years. Picked up a few tricks here and there. When you order shrimp cocktail, this is what they usually do, as its fast and they do it to order so there's no waste."

Isabella enjoyed watching Travis work. It was obvious that he enjoyed cooking and his motions were both smooth and effi-cient. He set a pot of water to boil and as soon as it started bubbling, he added half a bag of fettucine and lowered the heat. Meanwhile, he had a saute pan that he'd already added a hunk of butter and some olive oil to. He deftly minced a few garlic cloves and tossed those in, using an old wooden spoon to stir the garlic. A minute later, he added some sliced mushrooms. As soon as she could smell the enticing scent of the garlic, he added a handful of halved grape tomatoes and the shrimp to the pan and a sprinkle of red pepper flakes.

"It's almost ready now. The shrimp just take a few minutes. Are you getting hungry yet?"

"Starving! It smells amazing." Isabella's mouth was watering at the smell of the garlic and the sight of the shrimp, which were losing their translucence and starting to curl up a bit.

Less than ten minutes later, Travis took the pasta off the burner and drained out most of the water. He then added the pasta and a bit of the cooking water to the pan, along with a squeeze of fresh lemon juice, and then gave it a good stir. Within minutes, he handed her a full plate that smelled and looked amazing, and brought his own to the chair next to hers.

"Thank you! This beats the can of soup I probably would have heated up."

"You haven't tasted it yet," Travis teased as he got silverware, napkins and brought salt and pepper shakers over for them as well.

Once he was seated, Isabella twirled a bit of pasta and stabbed a piece of shrimp and took a bite. It was incredible.

"If the lawyer thing doesn't work out for you, you could always get restaurant work. This is such a treat. Thank you."

"Well, you did me a favor too. It's not nearly as much fun cooking something like this for one." Travis was relieved that she seemed to enjoy the dish. Every now and then as they ate, his leg brushed against hers and he wondered if she felt anything remotely like the reaction he felt just by being near her. Her hair looked gorgeous as it fell in thick waves to her shoulders and the smell of it was driving him crazy. When they finished eating, he put their plates in the sink and then asked, "Join me for a coffee on the deck? I love to sit out there after dinner and it's a gorgeous night."

"I never say no to coffee." Isabella looked relaxed and happy as she watched him make the coffee. When it was ready, they brought their cups out to the small deck off the living room and settled into the two bar-style chairs that were high enough to see over the railing.

"This was one of the reasons I chose this place. It's a small deck, but the views are great and it's just nice to sit outside, especially on a night like this."

"It's beautiful. Such a nice way to unwind after a long day. I have a patio at my place, but it's nice to be high up like this."

"We've known each other for so long, seventh-grade I think, right?" It amazed him that they'd been in each other's lives for so long, but always at a distance.

"Has it really been that long?" She frowned, remembering. "You weren't always very nice to me back then, if I recall."

Travis chuckled. "Do you mean the teasing? Or the bossing you around?"

"Both! I thought you were such a grouch back then. You didn't seem to like me at all," she laughed, remembering. "You always ordered me around whenever we were assigned to the same projects."

"That's what boys do when they like a girl at that age. It never was a good strategy."

"You had a crush on me then?" She looked at him then, shocked.

"Huge crush. Made me act like an idiot around you. I was in a shy stage."

"I had no idea. How come you never asked me out?"

"I wanted to. By the time I finally almost had the courage, it was tenth grade and you'd just become a cheerleader. You started dating Kenny Albright, star quarterback then, and I lost my window of opportunity."

"Kenny. I haven't thought of him in years. We dated all through high school and the first year of college, too, and then it fizzled out."

"It's probably good that we didn't date in high school, then. Those romances never seem to last."

"That's true." Isabella sipped her coffee and looked out at the view.

"I've never had the best timing," Travis admitted.

"What do you mean?"

"When we both moved back here after college, I wanted to ask you out then, but we'd both just started sort of working together and were trying to get our careers started. Then I met Ellen and we were together for a long time. Then, when we finally ended things, you were dating Christian. He never knew I was interested."

"I never knew, either. I didn't think of you that way, partly because you were Christian's best friend. Before that, it never crossed my mind because we did so much work together."

"Do you really think that matters, though? I don't think it has to."

"I don't know. What if we dated and then things didn't work out? It might be awkward," Isabella wondered out loud.

Travis had thought about that many times over the years.

"It doesn't have to be, though. We're both adults and we both like each other enough to handle that...although I'm thinking more positively that it could work out." Travis set his coffee cup down and held out his hand, and although her eyes were questioning, she did the same and put her hand in his. He pulled her up and into his arms.

"I've been dying to do this all night." He kissed her—softly, at first, and then as she melted into him, he deepened the kiss and cradled her head in his hands, kissing her gently before pulling back finally.

"I've been hoping you would, too," she admitted.

Travis's heart soared. "I want to take you on a real date, this weekend. If you're up for it?"

"I'd like that."

He pulled her in again for another kiss. He would have loved to kiss her all night, but knew they both had to be up early the next day and he didn't want to overwhelm her. So regretfully, after a few minutes, he pulled back and then walked her out to her car to say goodnight.

CHAPTER 16

Jolene, what an interesting night I had," Isabella told the small cat when she got home. Jolene responded with a curt meow and a flick of her fluffy tail, indicating she was more interested in what was for dinner. Isabella chuckled, fed her, then changed into her pajamas and crawled into bed, intending to read for a while before she went to sleep, but her thoughts kept returning to Travis.

She couldn't believe he'd been interested in her for so long and that she'd never had the slightest inkling. What did that say about her? She frowned, thinking back to Uncle Jim's comments at the wedding, wondering if she'd been too self-involved and focused on being successful to notice what was going on around her, to pick up on what Travis had been feeling. Maybe there were signs that she missed completely. She felt lucky that he was still interested, after all this time, and that he hadn't given up on her. She was definitely looking forward to getting to know him better. And, if she was being truthful, she couldn't wait to kiss him again. Their chemistry was off the charts and took her by surprise--it was so unexpected.

"YOUR TEN O'CLOCK APPOINTMENT, MRS. MAXWELL, IS HERE," Francie called from the front desk to let her know. Isabella walked out front to greet Uncle Jim's neighbor who had finally called to talk to her about listing her house for sale.

"Hello, Mrs. Maxwell, so nice to see you. Uncle Jim said he sees you often." Isabella led the elderly woman into one of the small meeting rooms and offered her coffee or tea as she settled into a comfy arm chair.

"I'd love a cup of tea, dear, if it's not too much trouble."

"Not at all. I'll be right back." She went to the kitchen area, made a cup of tea and then delivered it to Mrs. Maxwell.

Isabella took notes while Mrs. Maxwell sipped her tea and told her all about her house. She hated to sell, but it was getting to be too much for her and her best friend, Judy, loved living at the new assisted living center in town and thought maybe that would be a good idea for her, too.

"They have bingo every day, and no one has to drive anywhere. I admit, that sounds just wonderful to me."

"That sounds really fun, and relaxing, too," Isabella agreed and thought of Uncle Jim and how if he wasn't so feisty and independent, that he'd probably enjoy a place like that, too.

"The condos are so cute and all one level, so you don't have to deal with stairs, either."

"It sounds lovely," Isabella said with a smile.

Mrs. Maxwell took a sip of her tea and looked at Isabella for a moment, as if she was weighing what to say next. Finally she spoke. "I have to admit, you're not what I expected. I didn't think you'd be so friendly and nice."

Isabella's jaw fell open in surprise. She wasn't sure what to say to that.

Mrs. Maxwell kept talking, though, trying to explain, "It's

just that I haven't seen you in years, dear, and though your Uncle Jim thinks you hung the moon and the stars as he should, there was all that business with Molly and that bed and breakfast you opened."

Isabella cringed. Even though it had technically been Uncle Jim's idea, she should have known that it wasn't a good one. Opening a bed and breakfast so soon after Molly opened hers just made her look jealous and vindictive which, admittedly, she had been a bit.

"That wasn't one of my better decisions," Isabella admitted. "I did realize pretty quickly that it wasn't as easy as it appeared and that I didn't have the gift for it that Molly did, nor the experience. She did me a favor by taking it over."

"Everyone makes mistakes," Mrs. Maxwell said charitably. "You know, I almost called that other girl, Missy, as she's always been such a sweet little thing. But, your Uncle Jim reminded me that you have the experience and I'm glad that he did. You really do seem to know what you're doing."

"Thank you," Isabella said, and then they chatted some more about pricing and what needed to happen next. She walked Mrs. Maxwell through everything, and then promised to come by the next day to take pictures and put a nice ad together for her.

Once she was back at her desk, with a fresh cup of coffee in hand, she checked email and voicemail and was very pleasantly surprised to have a message from one of the homeowners she'd sent the mailing to that lived in Travis's favorite neighborhood. She called immediately, and after chatting for a few minutes made an appointment to go meet with them later that afternoon and discuss possibly listing their house.

Travis called as well while she was on the line with one of the homeowners and she called him back as soon as she finished the call.

"How's your morning going?" he asked after they'd exchanged hellos.

"Good, busy. I got a bite on the mailing I sent out, to your neighborhood."

"Really? Already?" He sounded impressed.

"Yes. I'm not sure how serious they are, but I'm going to meet with them this afternoon and hopefully might have a listing for you to look at later in the week."

"That's great. So, about later in the week. I wanted to confirm Saturday night with you. I thought we could go to dinner in Bozeman and maybe see a show."

"Sure, that sounds great."

"Good, it's a date then. I'll probably talk to you in a day or so."

"Okay, talk soon." Isabella hung up the phone and felt ridiculously happy. Her day was off to such a good start and she had a date lined up for the weekend.

THE HOUSE IN THE HILLS NEIGHBORHOOD WAS LOVELY, AND Isabella left with a signed listing in hand. Turned out her timing had been lucky as the owners were just about ready to sell their house when they'd received her letter. After seeing their home, she told the owners she had a buyer in mind, possibly several, and that she'd be in touch very shortly to schedule some showings.

She did have a buyer in mind, and she would be scheduling a showing for Travis, but she didn't think he would fall in love with this house. She knew an older couple that it would be perfect for as it was a smaller, bungalow style, just two bedrooms and all on one level. Still, she called Travis and he agreed that it was probably too small but he'd love to take a look anyway and wouldn't rule out the possibility of buying and remodeling to expand.

On the way back to the office, she stopped by the Muffin to grab a coffee for her and Anna. As she was walking in, Aidan was on his way out and smiled when he saw her.

"It's so good to see you. I've been meaning to call you," Aidan said and gave her a hug. It took her by surprise as she hadn't heard a thing from him since she'd last seen him when he mentioned heading back to New York for a visit.

"How was New York?" she asked.

"It was great. I've been meaning to call you to catch up. Are you free tonight? I'd love to buy you dinner and fill you in on why I disappeared for a bit."

Isabella's first impulse was to say no. She hadn't even thought of Aidan in days. But then she remembered her promise to Uncle Jim about giving him a second chance and to go out with him at least once if he asked. Still, she debated. It didn't quite feel right to her but then she told herself that was ridiculous. She and Travis hadn't even officially had their first date yet.

"Sure, I'd be happy to have dinner with you."

ISABELLA RETURNED TO THE OFFICE WITH THE COFFEES AND A small bag with a giant raspberry scone inside.

Anna was sitting at the front desk when she walked in, and her eyes lit up when she saw the coffee and the paper bag.

"What did you get?"

"Your favorite scone, so you have to help me eat it."

Anna sighed. "I really shouldn't, but I absolutely will. I've been dying for something sweet. We'll have to have it by your desk, though, so I can keep an eye on the front door. Francie is out running an errand."

Isabella handed her a coffee and then walked back to her desk as Anna followed and pulled up a chair. Missy was at her desk as well, in the middle of a call, and waved as they walked in. Isabella broke the scone in two and handed half to Anna, along with a paper napkin to catch the crumbs.

"So, have you heard from Travis about the weekend?" Anna asked. Isabella had filled her in on their night at his place and tentative plans to go out again.

"He called this morning and we're going out Saturday night. Dinner in Bozeman, or something." She paused for a moment and then said, "And I have a date tonight, too—with Aidan."

"You're going out with Aidan again?" Anna was shocked. "How did that come about?"

Isabella explained how she'd bumped into him at the Muffin. Missy was just ending her call, then and looked their way as she hung up the phone.

"Did you say you're seeing Aidan tonight? For a date?" she asked, and sounded a bit surprised as well.

"Yes. We're going to dinner, at Delancey's, I think."

"Really? Delancey's is really nice, great place for a date." Missy seemed a bit distracted as she gathered up her sweater, notebook and purse and shut down her computer.

"Are you gone for the day?" Anna asked.

"What? Oh, yes. I have a showing and am just going to head home after that. I'll see you both tomorrow." Missy rushed out then, and Isabella assumed she was running late for a meeting.

"She's been hard to figure, lately," Anna commented as Missy walked out the door.

"What do you mean?"

"In a great mood one day and then very quiet and withdrawn the next."

Isabella thought about that for a moment. "Well, she's been working really hard. Could be the ups and downs of this job. Things don't always go the way you expect. Or it may have something to do with Jeremy. she hasn't mentioned him in a while. Maybe things aren't going well."

"She and Jeremy broke up a few weeks ago. I thought you knew that."

Isabella was surprised. "No, I had no idea. She doesn't really share much with me, I guess. No wonder she's been moody then."

"Yeah, break-ups can be tough," Anna sympathized, and then shifted the conversation back to Isabella's date with Aidan. "So, what are you going to wear?"

ISABELLA DECIDED TO JUST STAY IN THE OUTFIT SHE'D BEEN wearing all day. It was perfectly fine and appropriate for Delancey's and she didn't feel like changing. She still had mixed feelings about this date. There was nothing wrong with going out to dinner with Aidan and she told herself that it was silly to feel guilty about it. But still, she did a bit. She wanted to get this date over with and to close the door completely on Aidan. But she thought of Uncle Jim again and sighed. She needed to be more open than that.

Aidan arrived at six sharp and they chatted easily on the drive to Delancey's.

"Traci did a great job with the decorating. It really feels like my place now," he said as they walked in to the restaurant. The hostess seated them, and a few minutes later their waitress came by for their drink orders and to tell them about the specials. Isabella ordered her usual soda water with lemon and Aidan a draft beer. Neither really had to look at the menu.

"I almost always get the steak when I come here," she admitted as Aidan stacked his menu on top of hers. The waitress returned with their drinks and they put their orders in.

They chatted for a few minutes and then Isabella said, "So tell me about your trip to New York. Was it bittersweet going back there? You must miss it." The waitress returned just then with a basket of rolls and their salads. Isabella reached for a roll as Aidan started talking.

"It was bittersweet, but not because I miss the city. I didn't go there alone," he said as he started to cut into his salad and then continued. "Missy came with me. We used to date, were pretty serious actually, before I moved to New York years ago. I never really got over her and wanted to start things up again when I moved back here, but she told me things were serious with Jeremy, so I backed off."

"You were serious with Missy?" Now her odd behavior of late made sense.

Aidan ran his hand through his hair, looking frustrated and a little sad. "She told me to move on and start dating other people. That's when I suggested we go out. I don't think Missy liked that idea much, but she couldn't really say anything against it if she was still with Jeremy." He paused for a minute to take a bite of his roll. "We ran into each other all the time and it was right after the weekend you and I went to the art festival in Bozeman that she came to see me and said she'd ended things with Jeremy."

"So you got back together?" Now she understood why she hadn't heard from Aidan. It hadn't just been a lack of chemistry after all.

"We did, and I thought it would be a romantic gesture to

bring her back to New York with me and introduce her to everyone there and show her around."

"It didn't go well?" Isabella guessed.

"It did, at first. She seemed to be having a great time and I was so proud to have her meet everyone. But on the plane ride home, she was very quiet and distant and I sensed that something was brewing, that she was bothered."

"What was it?" She was intrigued, wondering what Missy was thinking. It sounded like a dream weekend to her.

"She came over the next night and said she had slept on it, and woke up knowing that we weren't right for each other after all. She saw in New York that we were too different, that I had moved on to a place that she couldn't go. It was too much for her. She thinks I should move back to New York. She's convinced that's where I belong and there's no place for her in my world. I tried to tell her she was way off base, that I'd just bought a house here, for God's sake, but she said it was easier for her to just end things now, before she got in too deep again."

"She's afraid that you'll leave her again." Isabella understood now.

"I think so, yes." The happy spark that had been in his eyes when they first got to Delancey's had dimmed as he picked at his salad.

"Well, how long has it been? Maybe she'll come around."

"I don't think so. She told me that night to move on and start dating other people and that she was going to do the same."

"Is she getting back with Jeremy?" Isabella wondered.

"I don't think so. If he was right for her, she never would have ended things. She's not like that." Isabella wondered about that. Not about Jeremy, but about Aidan. It was clear to her that he was madly in love with Missy and it sounded like she felt the same, but was just scared, terrified, and over-whelmed by who Aidan had become and what his life was like in New York.

"So, I thought I owed you an explanation at least, and I don't know if you'd consider going out again, but I really did have fun with you." He spoke half-heartedly, and although he attempted a smile, it didn't reach his eyes.

"I agreed to come to dinner with you because I was curious to hear what you had to say. I think you're a great guy, Aidan, but I think we both know that we're meant to just be friends," She smiled then and Aidan just looked even more sad, and also maybe a bit relieved.

Isabella leaned forward. The solution seemed obvious to her. "Do you love her?" she asked.

Aidan nodded miserably, and Isabella smiled. "Here's what I think you should do."

CHAPTER 17

There's a Bethany Evans on the phone," Mrs. Crosby called to him. "Should I put her through?" Travis hesitated for a moment. He hadn't expected to hear from Bethany any time soon, but maybe it was a legal issue.

"Sure, put her through." He picked up the line. "This is Travis."

"Hi, Travis, it's Bethany. How are you?" Her voice was sugary sweet and the sound of her drawl grated on his nerves. He was already having a stressful day, and this didn't help.

"I'm fine, thanks. How can I help you?" he asked politely.

"Well, I know you're working so I'll keep it brief, but I just wanted to say hello and invite you to a little gathering I'm having this weekend. It's a charity event, actually, to benefit the food pantry."

"That's nice of you. I'll check with Isabella. I know she'll appreciate that it's for the food pantry."

"You're dating Isabella?" The tone of her voice wasn't quite as sweet and she actually sounded surprised.

"Yes, we're officially dating now," he said with a chuckle.

"Oh, I didn't know. I assumed she was back with Aidan," she said.

"Why would you think that?" he asked, and found himself dreading her response.

Bethany hesitated for a minute and then said, "Well, I was having a drink at the bar at Delancey's last night and saw her having dinner with Aidan. They were in such an intense conversation or I would have gone over to say hello, but I didn't want to interrupt."

Travis was silent for a moment, and then said, "Oh. Well, maybe they were discussing real estate. I know she just sold him a place recently." That didn't make a lot of sense to him, but he didn't know what else to say; he just wanted to get off the phone.

"Maybe. I don't know." She sounded doubtful.

"I need to run, but will let you know about the party. Thank you for the invite."

Travis hung up the phone, and after ten minutes of stewing, he called the one person he could talk to about this. Traci answered on the first ring.

"Hey, stranger," she laughed.

Travis got right to the point. "Are you free for lunch? I need to talk to you."

"Sure thing. Meet at the Muffin at noon?" she suggested.

"Perfect, see you there."

HIS SISTER WAS ALREADY AT THE MORNING MUFFIN WHEN HE walked in and she waved him over.

She gave him a big hug and then they both sat down.

"It was mobbed when I got here so I went ahead and ordered for you. I hope turkey is okay?" Traci had found them a quiet table in the corner and had a turkey sandwich, chips and a coke waiting for him. She was the best.

"Thank you. This is what I probably would have ordered." He smiled and she teased him a little. "Yeah, they do have sandwiches that aren't turkey you know. You should really venture out of your comfort zone one of these days."

"I probably should," he agreed, and took a big bite of the sandwich. "But when I find something I like, I tend to stick with it."

Traci started on her sandwich as well and then after a few minutes, she set it down and looked directly at her brother.

"So, what's going on? Why did you need to talk to me right away?" She sounded both curious and concerned.

Travis filled her in on his conversation with Bethany.

"Are you sure she's telling the truth?" was her immediate response. She was not a fan of the Southern Belle.

"Yeah, I do. She was a bit too happy about what she'd seen. It sounded genuine."

Traci frowned. "But you had a great time the other night and she sounded excited to go out on Saturday?"

Travis nodded. "I wouldn't think much of it, but she did have a pretty big crush on him for a while. She even went kayaking because of him."

"Actually, she went kayaking because of you," Traci corrected him.

"Well, technically, but I trained her so she could be safe out there. I didn't realize it was because of him."

"You should talk to her. Things aren't always what they seem. And if they are, well, better to know now, right?"

Travis thought about that for a minute and reluctantly agreed.

"Right. I'll talk to her, before Saturday. I think we have a showing tomorrow afternoon."

"Good, get it out of the way so you can have a great night on Saturday."

"You're so optimistic." He wished he shared her enthusiasm.

"Well, I know you. Aidan's not remotely right for her, and she's a smart girl. She'll see that."

———

MISSY BARELY SPOKE, LET ALONE LOOKED ISABELLA'S WAY THE following day and Isabella just shrugged it off, guessing that Aidan hadn't had a chance to talk to her yet and smooth things out. The next morning, however, was a very different story. Isabella arrived later than usual due to an early client meeting and found Missy surrounded by all the women in the office. As she walked closer, she heard her say, "And so he quoted my favorite movie of all time, 'When Harry Met Sally'. He got down on one knee and said, "When you find the person you want to spend the rest of your life with, you want the rest of your life to start right away. And then he asked me to marry him. He really wants to stay here, in Beauville, with me."

Isabella smiled at the wonder and excitement in her voice. She walked over to the group and Missy looked up as she got near.

"Sounds like congratulations are in order," Isabella said.

Missy rushed over and gave her a hug. "Thank you so much. Aidan said you've been a really good friend to him, and encouraged him to do this. I had no idea."

"Let me see it," Isabella demanded and then drew her breath in at the sight of the lovely, cushion cut diamond. "Oh, it's beautiful."

"Thank you. I'm just so happy." She dabbed at her eyes, which were watering as she laughed nervously. "I can't believe

I'm crying, again. I've been like waterworks ever since he asked me."

"Do you have any idea when you'll get married?" Anna asked.

"If it was up to Aidan, it would be this week, at the town hall. But my mother would kill me if I did that. We're going to do something small, in about a month or so. My mother is feverishly starting on it now."

She turned to Isabella. "I'm moving into to his place tomorrow. Our place," she corrected herself.

"I'm really happy for you," Isabella said sincerely, and then added, "He's really crazy about you, you know."

"I guess he is. And I feel the same. It's pretty amazing."

Someone came in the front door then, as another phone rang and everyone went back to work. Isabella poured herself a fresh cup of coffee and settled in at her desk to go through email. There was a message from another one of the home-owners in the hills, wanting to schedule an initial appointment to discuss listing their house. Isabella looked up the address for this one and a little thrill went through her. It was too soon to say for sure, but this one looked more up Travis's alley. It was a newer home and seemed to have everything he was looking for. She set an appointment to meet with the owners the next day, and then the rest of her day flew until Travis arrived at three thirty to go look at the first listing in the neighborhood he liked.

Anna buzzed her when Travis arrived and she walked out to greet him.

"Hi, are you ready to go?" he asked. There were no compliments and she'd worn one of favorite dresses, made from a deep, purple-blue fabric that shimmered when the light hit it and made her hair look almost black. It was an outfit that always made her feel good when she wore it.

"Yes, I'll just grab my bag and we can go."

When they walked outside, she hesitated and asked, "Okay for me to drive, or would you prefer to?" She sensed that he was in a strange mood.

"You can drive," he said, as if he didn't care much one way or the other.

The drive to the house was quiet and somewhat tense. Isabella attempted some easy chit-chat, and after a few one word answers, she gave up and drove the rest of the way in silence.

The house had a lockbox on it, so she punched in the combination, took out the key and let them in. The house was adorable, a classic bungalow with lovely, large windows that offered panoramic views of the valley and town below. The house was meticulously maintained and very pretty, but definitely small. Isabella showed him through the rest of the house and then as they walked out, asked him what he thought. He hadn't said a word as they looked around.

"It's too small," he said dismissively as they got back into Isabella's car.

"I thought that it might be," she agreed. "But you did mention the possibility of remodeling and building out."

He shook his head. "No, I don't want to invest that much time and effort for an unknown result. I'll keep looking. I'll know it when I see it, I think."

"Okay." They rode back to the office in silence and Isabella wondered what was going on with Travis. He'd always been kind of moody; maybe he was having a bad day.

"How's your day been going?" she asked tentatively.

"Fine. Busy, as usual."

She pulled into her office parking lot and then Travis turned to her. "Are we still on for Saturday night?" He sounded doubtful and even a bit angry and Isabella didn't know what to think.

"Yes, why wouldn't we be? I'm looking forward to it."

Travis was quiet for a minute and then said, "Are you sure? You wouldn't rather go out with Aidan?"

Isabella quickly put two and two together. Someone had obviously seen her out with Aidan.

"Aidan is my friend, and he and Missy got engaged last night. I encouraged him to go for it."

Whatever Travis was expecting to hear, that wasn't it.

"He's engaged? To Missy?"

"Yes, and they're madly in love."

"Oh, okay. So, I guess I'll see you Saturday then?" He smiled then, a somewhat sheepish, mostly relieved smile that lit up his face and made his dimples dance.

Impulsively, Isabella reached up and gave him a quick kiss.

"I can't wait to go out Saturday. See you then."

CHAPTER 18

I sabella was nervous. Travis was due to pick her up in fifteen minutes and she still wasn't dressed. She was staring at the clothes hanging in her walk-in closet as Jolene did figure eights around her ankles.

"I already fed you. What is up with you?" The little cat continued to purr and rub against her leg.

"Well, make yourself useful, then. What should I wear?" Jolene meowed in response and Isabella sighed. She had a million things to wear, but nothing seemed right and she'd been standing there for almost ten minutes now, willing something to jump out at her as the perfect choice. Finally, it came to her.

She wasn't sure exactly where they were going. Travis had mentioned something about dinner and maybe a show. She reached for a dress that was tucked way in the back of her closet. She hadn't worn it in ages, but it had always been a favorite and it was very flattering. It was a basic black cocktail dress with a sophisticated, gathered halter top, a nipped waist and slightly flared skirt that just reached her knees. It had a retro Breakfast at Tiffany's look to it, and when she pulled it on and checked her reflection in the mirror she felt a bit like Audrey Hepburn. It was a great dress.

She decided to wear a cute pair of candy apple red pumps and a string of pearls. An extra coat of black mascara and a slick of deep red lipstick, and she was finally ready just as there was a knock on the door.

She came downstairs and opened the door and Travis stood there, looking so handsome that it took her breath away. He was wearing a nice, navy jacket over tan khakis and a pale green dress shirt. He smiled and handed her a pretty bouquet of gerbera daisies that were a rainbow of vivid colors.

"I thought of you when I saw these. I hope you like daisies."

"They're beautiful, thank you." She brought the flowers into the kitchen and set them on the island.

"Ready to head out?" He looked eager to go.

TRAVIS DROVE, AND A HALF-HOUR LATER THEY WERE IN Bozeman. One of his clients had recommended a new restaurant that also had an attached club that featured local bands. After an amazing dinner, they went next door to the club and Travis had a reserved cocktail table near the stage. Tonight, they were featuring The Bridger Mountain Big Band, a huge, seventeen-piece band that played a mix of jazz and blues. Because it felt like a special occasion, Isabella ordered a special coffee drink that had Tia Maria liqueur in it and a mound of whipped cream on top with a drizzle of chocolate. Travis got an aged scotch over ice.

They settled in to listen to the music and Travis draped his arm across the back of her chair. The band was wonderful and Isabella sighed in contentment. They couldn't really talk until the band took a break and the waitress came by to see if they wanted more drinks. Isabella asked for a water and Travis still had more than half his scotch left.

"How did you ever find a band like this in Bozeman? I feel like we should be in an underground nightclub in New York City, and I should be wearing a flapper dress!"

Travis chuckled at that. "I like the dress you have on. You look amazing." He brushed her hair gently to the side and leaned in for a kiss. It only lasted a moment, but it took her by surprise and she wished it didn't have to end. "I've been dying to do that all night," he admitted. The band started getting back into position, signaling that they were about to begin their second set. "Oh, and this band has played in Bozeman for years. They have quite a following. It's the first time I've seen them, though."

They stayed through the second set and then decided to head home. Isabella couldn't believe that she was out with Travis and it felt like they'd been together forever. She was so comfortable with him, but what they had was so much more powerful than friendship. His hand was resting lightly on her thigh and the touch was driving her crazy. She couldn't wait to get home and into his arms.

She didn't even have to invite him in. It was a given that he was coming inside, and as soon as she unlocked the front door and they stepped inside, he pulled her into his arms.

"I thought we'd never get here," he whispered in her ear and he trailed kisses across her face until he reached her lips. She sank into him and ran her hands through the thick hair at the nape of his neck.

"Let's go to the couch and get more comfortable," she suggested when they came up for air again. "Do you want anything to drink?"

"No, I don't need anything. Just you." He led her to the sofa and pulled her down next to him and back into his arms. They kissed off and on for about an hour before Isabella finally yawned and Travis took that as his cue to go. She really didn't want him to leave, but it seemed too soon to invite him to stay.

"I'll call you tomorrow, see what you're up to."

Isabella had been planning to set up a showing for the new listing in the Hills for Travis on Monday or Tuesday, but it sounded like he might be free on Sunday.

"I could try and set up a showing for you tomorrow afternoon if you're not busy and would rather see it then."

"I don't want to make you work on your day off," Travis protested.

Isabella laughed. "Are you kidding? This is fun for me. I'm excited for you to see this one."

"Well, if you're sure you don't mind?"

"I'll try to set it up for tomorrow afternoon."

ISABELLA SLEPT IN THE NEXT DAY AND THEN PUT A CALL IN around ten to the homeowners in the Hills to see if it would be okay to show the house that afternoon. They agreed to a two o'clock showing and Isabella confirmed it. She'd just poured herself a second cup of coffee when the phone rang and it was Travis.

"Did you sleep okay?" he asked.

"Like a baby," she chuckled. "Thanks again for a wonderful night and for the flowers. They looked so pretty when I came downstairs this morning."

"It was my pleasure. I had a great time, too. I had a feeling I would." How had she never really noticed the rich deepness of his voice before? Now just the sound of it made her smile. She definitely had it bad.

"I reached the owners. They said a showing at two was good for them."

"Great. Why don't I swing by your place a little before and we can head over."

Isabella took a long, hot shower and then puttered around the rest of the day, doing laundry and killing time until Travis knocked on her door a little after one thirty.

He drove, and then when they were almost there, he asked,"Is this the one?" as they came around the corner and reached a long driveway.

"Yes. It's a double-lot, two acres, and is very private."

Travis turned onto the driveway and the let out a low whistle as the house came into view.

"Wow," he said, and Isabella smiled. It was impressive from the outside but was even better inside. She couldn't wait to show it to him.

She opened the door and they walked in to a foyer with a cathedral ceiling and light streaming in from all the windows. The style was a rustic contemporary with lots of light, polished wood and floor to ceiling windows everywhere. The view across the valley and town below was magnificent. She led him into the kitchen and his smile grew even wider. He reminded her of the proverbial kid in the candy store.

The kitchen had all the bells and whistles—stainless steel appliances, snowy, white wood cabinets, honed Carrara marble countertops and a V-shaped island with chairs on either side, with a stovetop in the center, so he could cook and chat with guests. He ran his hand reverently over the cool marble.

"This is amazing."

"You haven't seen anything yet. Come downstairs." She led him into the basement which was finished and had a big screen TV, and a mini-kitchen and bar. There was also plenty of room for a pool table. Travis walked all around the room and

Isabella guessed that he was mentally seeing himself there. His expression was far off and dreamy.

"Ready to see the bedrooms?"

"Lead the way."

The second floor had four bedrooms, all good-sized, including the master bedroom which was huge. There was also a small deck as well as an oversized bathroom with a Jacuzzi tub and not one, but two large walk-in closets.

"His and her closets. Very nice," Travis commented.

When they came back downstairs, she showed him the office around the corner, next to the formal dining room. The office had custom-made, built-in bookcases and two desks, with matching chocolate brown leather chairs. The room was big enough that two people could work there easily and Isabella explained that the current owners often did that. One worked from home full-time and the other was about to retire, which is why they were interested in selling. They wanted to downsize to something smaller and all one level.

"What do you think?" Travis asked as he looked around the office.

"I'd love an office like this." Isabella currently had a small desk in her spare bedroom but didn't have a dedicated home office. Even if she wasn't working, this room would be a great one to curl up and read in. It had the feel of a library or den as well as an office.

"There's a three-car garage and a big patio out back with a fire-pit. The owners told me they often had family over and their grandchildren loved when they built a fire and everyone gathered around it," Isabella shared as Travis ran his hand over the smooth mahogany wood.

"What did you say the asking price is on it again?"

Isabella told him and he nodded. "That seems about right. It's a little higher than I wanted to go, but it's possible."

He walked back into the family room, which opened up to the kitchen area. It was a spacious room, with gleaming hardwood floors and a gas fireplace in the corner. Isabella could picture a roaring fire going while Travis whipped up something amazing in the kitchen and she and their friends gathered around the island. It was the perfect house for him.

"Do you like this one better than the other one, the one with the pool table?" Travis asked and seemed very interested in her answer.

"Well, that's a nice house, too, but it doesn't really matter which one I like, it's your decision. You can't go wrong either way."

"Okay, forget you are my realtor. I just want your opinion. If you were buying the house, which one would you go with?"

Isabella didn't even hesitate. "This one, absolutely. The other house was great, too, but if I bought this one I don't think I'd ever want to move again."

Travis grinned at that. "I know what you mean. Let me sleep on this tonight and I'll call you tomorrow, probably to put an offer together for this one."

He walked over to her then and wrapped his arms around her. "Is it okay to kiss my realtor now?" He didn't wait for an answer, just pulled her in tight and kissed her so thoroughly that she didn't want to let go.

CHAPTER 19

Isabella got up early the next morning to bake. She didn't cook much, but she did know how to make the best chocolate chip cookies. While in college, she had worked part-time at a famous cookie shop near campus. The store had locations all over the U.S., and although Isabella had gained ten pounds during her time working there, she did learn the secret to making a good cookie and how to make lots of variations from the same dough.

Cold butter, that was the key. She cut the right amount of butter from the stick and then added it to her mixer along with the rest of the ingredients and let it go just until the butter was evenly incorporated. For this batch, she was adding a scoop of creamy peanut butter to make peanut butter chocolate chip cookies that would melt in Travis's mouth. She was going to bring them into the office to celebrate the signing of the purchase and sale agreement. It had been two weeks since his offer had been accepted and if all went well, they would be closing in a little over a month.

She got ready for work while the several sheets of cookies baked. After letting them cool for a bit while she dried her hair, she packed them carefully in a plastic container and then left for the office. As she drove in, she thought about how happy she was and how she and Travis had spent almost every day or night together since their first official date. He'd had her over several times for dinner at his place and she'd returned the favor at her place with takeout or pizza delivery. Things were going so well, it was as if they'd been together for years instead of just a few weeks. She thought back to a conversation she'd had with Anna earlier in the week when she'd asked how things were going.

"It's just easy. It feels right and the spark is still so strong. Honestly, it's never been like this for me." Isabella's past relationships hadn't been this easy ever; there was always something off-balance that made things stressful at times. It was almost too easy with Travis. She couldn't help but think it was too good to last. She shared this fear with Anna, who just laughed.

"Don't be silly. That is exactly as it should be. Love isn't supposed to be hard."

TRAVIS CAME BY THE OFFICE MID-MORNING TO SIGN THE purchase and sales agreement and Isabella had reserved the conference room for them. Once the paperwork was out of the way, she handed him a container of cookies.

"You made these, for me? Seriously?" He took one out and bit into it, finished the cookie a moment later and the reached for another. "These are amazing. I thought you said you didn't cook?"

"I don't," Isabella laughed. "I can bake cookies and make dip, that's about it."

Travis leaned over and gave her a quick kiss before saying,

"Well, you do both very well. You can bake for me any time." He had to head back to the office, but they had plans to meet up right after work, at Delancey's, to celebrate. Traci and Dan as well as Molly and Christian were meeting them there for drinks and dinner.

THEY HAD A GREAT TIME AT DELANCEY'S. AFTER MEETING AT the bar for a drink, they were soon after seated at a large round table, and once everyone had ordered they caught up with each other. Molly's bed and breakfast business was booming, Christian was as busy as ever and was starting on a new development of affordable homes for first-time buyers, Dan was completely settled in and said he was surprised by how little he missed Chicago and Traci was starting to cut back her hours at Snow's department store to part-time, because her decorating business had grown so much. But Traci had the most exciting news of all. "We're pregnant! With twins."

Congratulations rang around the table and then Isabella whispered to Travis, "Did you know about this?"

"Yes, she told me a week ago and swore me to secrecy. I've been dying to tell you."

Molly looked at Christian and asked, "I know Traci's a twin, but do they run in your family, too? Should I be nervous?" To which Christian just laughed, and said, "Not that I know of, but twins would be fine with me."

The night had been a lively one, but Travis had seemed a little quieter than usual. Isabella chalked it up to a long week, and buying a house was always more stressful than people realized. He'd also told her that he had to make it an early night as he had to work in the morning, even though it was a Saturday and she wouldn't be seeing him tomorrow night, either, as he was going to some kind of work thing in Bozeman. He'd told her about it earlier in the week, a golf tournament maybe. Isabella didn't mind, though. She hadn't stayed in on a Saturday night in a while and was looking forward to having a movie night and just relaxing.

Once they'd settled the check, she excused herself to use the ladies' room. Delancey's was packed by then, and by this time the bar was even busier than the restaurant. Bethany was fixing her makeup in the mirror as Isabella walked in. She nodded hello and then resumed talking to a woman that Isabella didn't know. Her ears perked up, though, when she heard Bethany mention Travis.

"Yeah, he's here with is realtor. Uh-huh, the tall one with the dark hair. We talk all the time. He seemed excited about my event tomorrow when I invited him. I can't wait to see him again."

The other woman murmured something and Isabella couldn't quite catch what she said. She heard low laughter, and then it was quiet again. When she came out of the stall, Bethany and her friend were gone. She told herself it was nothing; she must have heard wrong. Travis wouldn't still be talking to Bethany, and if he was going to a charity event of hers he would have invited her. But, he hadn't mentioned any such event. He also wasn't going to be seeing him the following night. Could his work thing be Bethany's charity event?

She couldn't decide what was more upsetting, the thought of him not telling her about this event and going without her, or her even wondering if he was hiding something from her. She did know that she didn't trust Bethany for a minute.

Travis was waiting by the front door for her and they headed out to their cars. They'd come straight from work but both assumed that he'd either be coming back to her place or that she would be going to his. Isabella wasn't ready for either option until she talked to him.

"Is something wrong?" He asked as they walked outside. Isabella knew her face was like an open book, when she was upset or mad it was obvious.

"Have you been talking to Bethany?" she asked?

That seemed to take him by surprise. "Bethany?"

"Yes, Bethany. Did she invite you to some charity event at her house tomorrow?"

He was quiet for a minute, which made Isabella all the more anxious. He was hiding something.

"Yes, she did, but..."

"And you didn't think to mention it? It's tomorrow right. Are you going?"

"No, I'm not going. I'm going to Bozeman, I told you that."

"Yes, that's what you said. But you never did mention that you talked to her or that she invited you to her house."

"Are you accusing me of something?" He was starting to get angry now, too, and defensive, which only pissed off Isabella even more.

"I don't know, am I? You've been a grump all night. Maybe you're feeling guilty about something."

"This is ridiculous. I'm going home. I'll call you tomorrow when you've come to your senses."

"Fine, go home. Have fun at Bethany's!" Isabella got in her car and slammed the door. The tears started flowing as she drove and she realized it had been a long week for her, too. She was home ten minutes later, scooped up a purring Jolene who was waiting at the door to greet her and headed upstairs to climb into her pajamas and fall into bed. She fell asleep within minutes of her head hitting the pillow.

CHAPTER 20

The phone woke Isabella up at a little past eight. She guessed it was Travis as she reached for the phone, but then smiled as she saw from the Caller ID that it was Uncle Jim.

"Good morning," she answered.

"Whatcha doing?" Uncle Jim asked, full of energy and sounding like he'd already been up for hours. Given the time, he probably had. Uncle Jim was an early-riser.

"Being lazy, thinking about getting out of bed."

"Well, do it and come over right now. I just took a coffee cake out of the oven and I can't eat it all myself." Isabella hadn't seen Uncle Jim in almost two weeks as she'd had to miss their most recent family dinner. An Uncle Jim fix was exactly what she needed.

"Will do. I'll be right over." She slid out of bed, dressed quickly, then fed Jolene and headed out the door to Uncle Jim's. She smiled when she saw her sister Jen's car in the driveway. So she had been summoned, too.

"Both of my favorite girls are here now," he called out as

Isabella stepped into the kitchen. "Pour yourself a coffee and grab a slice. We'll go into the sun room."

They did as he directed and everyone got comfortable in the sun room. Isabella took a sip of coffee. It was a rich, dark roast and tasted as good as it smelled. The coffee cake was still warm and the combination was exactly what she needed.

"So, what's new? Fill me in on your lives," Uncle Jim commanded.

Jen spoke first. "I'm heading back to Ireland soon, in two weeks, to do some more research for my next book. I may visit a castle in Scotland, too."

Uncle Jim took a big bite of cake and was quiet for a moment before addressing Jen. "So, would that research have a name? Ian, perhaps?"

Jen laughed. "It just might."

Satisfied with her answer, Uncle Jim turned his attention to Isabella. "And what about you, young lady? You're too quiet."

"Well, I thought things were going really great with Travis. It seemed too good to be true," Isabella said.

"Explain," Uncle Jim demanded.

Isabella filled them in on her run-in with Bethany. Jen immediately made a face. "I wouldn't believe one word that she says." Then in surprise, she added, "You don't, do you?"

"No, I don't think that I do. I was upset last night, but more at her than at him. Though I didn't realize that at the time." She took a long sip of coffee and then continued. "I'd been lying in bed thinking about it when you called. I don't think there's anything to it. Travis has never given me any reason to doubt him. It's funny, I was just saying to Anna yesterday that so far everything with Travis has just been so easy, no drama at all. No worrying or wondering how he feels." She took another sip of coffee and the added, "Anna said that's the way it's supposed to be."

"It is," Uncle Jim agreed.

"It's just that it's never been like that for me before. It was difficult for me to accept that it's real and that it will stay that way."

"When you find the right person, that's exactly how it is. You just know, and it feels right and easy and you feel better when you're around them."

"Is that how it was with you and Aunt Helen?"

"Always. We had the occasional fight, of course, everyone does. But it was always over silly things and we always made up fast. Making up was a lot of fun, actually." He smiled then, remembering.

"It hasn't been that long, though, for us. We've only been dating for a few weeks."

"You've known Travis forever, though," Jen said.

"A few weeks, forever, it's all the same. When it's right, it's right," Uncle Jim said as he got up to get another slice of cake.

"You should call him," Jen said while Uncle Jim was in the kitchen.

Isabella had been thinking the same thing. "I definitely over-reacted. I'll call him on the way home."

Uncle Jim came back with another slice for each of them. "So, have we figured everything out now? You know what to do?"

"Yes, I think we're good."

"I like him, you know. He's good for you."

"I know. I think so, too."

ISABELLA CALLED TRAVIS AS SOON AS SHE PULLED OUT OF Uncle Jim's driveway and started to head home. His phone rang once and then went right into voicemail, meaning he probably had it turned off. She left a quick message that simply said, "I'm sorry. Call me when you can."

She spent the rest of the afternoon doing laundry and grocery shopping. She'd picked up a rotisserie chicken at the market and a carton of Ben and Jerry's Cherry Garcia ice cream, as a special treat. She'd finished dinner and a generous scoop of ice cream and was debating between two on-demand movies when her phone rang and it was Travis.

"Hi, what are you up to?" she asked.

"Well, I think it's rude to just drop by so I'm calling first to see if it's okay to come over?"

"I thought you had something in Bozeman?"

"I got out early. So, are you up for company?"

"Yes, of course. Come on over."

"Good. Open the door."

"What?"

"Open the door. Like I said, I didn't want to just drop by. I'm calling first," he said with a chuckle.

Isabella jumped up and opened the door. Travis was standing there, wearing a huge grin and holding a bouquet of gorgeous red roses.

"You got these for me?" she said softly. "They're beautiful."

"Who else would they be for?" he teased her.

"Come in, you're getting wet." It was starting to mist outside as Isabella pulled him inside and he handed her the flowers. She brought them to the kitchen, found a vase to put them in and then brought them back to the living room. She set them on the coffee table where she look at them and smell them.

"Want some ice cream? I have a fresh carton of Cherry Garcia."

"You haven't had any yet? How is that possible?"

"Well, maybe just a little, but I'll join you and have a bit more." He nodded and she scooped some ice cream into a bowl for him, adding more to her dish as well. She brought the ice cream over to the sofa where Travis had just sat down and curled up next to him, handing him his bowl.

After a bite or two, Travis said, "Bethany did call me, that much was true. She invited me to that charity event of hers and said it was for the food pantry. I told her I'd check with you first, to see if you wanted to go and she didn't like that. That's when she told me that she'd just seen you having dinner with Aidan. I didn't enjoy that phone call too much, let me tell you."

So Bethany was the one who had seen her with Aidan. That figured. She probably couldn't wait to call Travis and thought she could worm her way back in.

"I didn't mention it to you because I didn't think you'd be interested in going and I certainly had no desire to. To be honest, once you set me straight about Aidan, I forgot all about Bethany and her stupid party."

"I was just thinking things were going almost too perfectly with us, that it was too good to be true, so her timing couldn't have been better, really, as I was feeling a little insecure, and I over-reacted."

"You think things are too good to be true with us?" Travis was looking at her intently.

"Yes. No. I just hope it stays like this," Isabella said softly.

"It will. It's meant to be, you and me. We're pretty perfect together." He set his empty bowl on the coffee table, next to hers and pulled her close to him.

"I love you, Isabella Graham." He kissed her gently on the forehead and then on each cheek before cradling her head in his hands and finally kissing her mouth, lightly at first, but then he quickly deepened the kiss until Isabella pulled back and looked him in the eye.

"I am madly in love with you, Travis Jones," she said, and then leaned in to kiss him again.

"I'm glad we got that sorted out," he said a short while later, when they both came up for air.

"Do you want to head upstairs? We might be more comfortable?"

"Lead the way. I'll follow you anywhere."

THE FOLLOWING SATURDAY, ISABELLA AND TRAVIS GOT UP early and Travis drove over to Uncle Jim's to pick up the kayak that Isabella had borrowed before. Uncle Jim was there to greet them and was in an unusually enthusiastic mood.

"I'm so glad you decided to step out of your comfort zone and try this kayaking thing again. Going down that river sounds like quite an adventure," Uncle Jim said when they came into the sun room to say hello before grabbing the kayak. Isabella wasn't as excited as Uncle Jim, though. Travis had suggested earlier in the week that they do a longer river trip that Sunday and she had agreed to go, but admitted that she was a little nervous. When he suggested they do another session in the pool the day before, to go over the safety moves again and practice rolling, she was more than happy to do so. She thought she remembered, but since she'd only gone that one time, it did seem like a good idea to have another practice session.

Travis grabbed the kayak and threw it in the back of the truck and then they said goodbye to Uncle Jim.

"Let me know how it goes," he called after them, and they agreed to give a full report when they returned.

When they arrived at the pool, it was still early and they had it completely to themselves. Travis dropped the kayaks in the pool. They jumped in and Travis showed her a few different moves. Then he asked her to do a roll to see if she could remember the move. She took a deep breath, focused and then, using all her strength and her hips, she swung the kayak over and back up.

"I did it!" She was surprised that her first try had been a success.

"Good job. Okay, watch mine."

He went to flip his, but then Isabella sneezed and missed it. A minute later he was back up and staring at her oddly.

"Did you see my roll."

"Sure, it was good."

"Really? You saw the whole thing?" He was looking at her so strangely.

"Well, no. I saw the beginning, but then I sneezed and didn't actually see the whole thing."

Travis looked relieved. "Okay, I'll do it again. Pay close attention and don't take your eyes off the kayak."

"Okay, go ahead."

He still had such an odd, almost hopeful expression on his face as he swung his kayak over and up and this time she saw what he wanted her to see. On the bottom of his kayak, in silver duct tape, he'd spelled out the words, "Marry Me?"

He flipped back up and looked at her expectantly. But she could hardly see them, her eyes were so filled with tears.

"Well?" he asked.

"Oh, my God," was all she was able to say.

"So you saw the bottom of the kayak?"

She nodded. He paddled over to her and reached out his hand. She put her hand in his, and then he said, "Isabella Graham, it is almost too good to be true with us. But I like to think we're just meant to be. I want to grow old with you, to sit around eating Cherry Garcia ice cream with you for the rest of our lives. If you'll have me. Will you marry me?"

"Yes, yes, of course I will!"

He reached deep beside him in the kayak and pulled a small plastic bag out of a side compartment. In the bag was a small square box, and Isabella held her breath, dying to see what was in the box and terrified that it might fall into the pool. Travis carefully opened the box and lifted a delicate diamond ring out of it and then slid the ring onto her finger. Once it was safely in place, she sighed with relief and looked at the ring in awe. It was a beautiful, cushion cut diamond surrounded by a circle of tiny diamonds. It took her breath away.

"Uncle Jim is going to love this story," she said.

"He thought it was a great idea. I chatted with him a few days ago and he fully approved," Travis admitted with a chuckle.

"I bet he did. No wonder he was in such a good mood this morning."

"Want to go give him the good news? We can make the rounds and tell everyone."

"That sounds like a perfect plan to me. Have I mentioned that I love you, Mr. Jones?"

"I love you, too, Miss Graham. Oh, and we don't really have to go kayaking tomorrow if you don't want to. I just said that so we'd have a reason to come here."

Isabella laughed. "Maybe we should put off the kayaking until next summer. I have a wedding to plan."

EPILOGUE

"This is a lot of house for two people," Uncle Jim said as Travis and Isabella showed him around their new house, and Jolene followed them from room to room. Travis had closed a week earlier and had surprised Isabella by putting her name on the deed as well. They were due to be married in a few months, but Travis had insisted that she move in when he did so it would truly feel like their place.

"Well, it might not be just the two of us for long. Twins do run in the family, you know," Travis teased.

"You're not expecting yet?" Uncle Jim asked and sounded more hopeful than shocked.

"No, of course not, Uncle Jim! Travis, really." She shook her head at him and he just laughed.

"Well, they do, and if I have my way, it won't be long," Travis said with a grin.

Isabella ignored that and asked, "Uncle Jim, can we get you anything to drink?"

He thought about that a moment and then said, "I'll have a

Kahlua and milk, if you have it. Not too strong, though. I have to drive, you know."

Isabella smiled at that. Uncle Jim wasn't much of a drinker at all. She'd never seen him have more than one.

Within minutes, the rest of their families and good friends had arrived. Isabella knew that Travis had been dying to have a housewarming party and was thrilled when she let him know it was all set, and that everyone would be over soon. Traci had helped them settle in this past week, and brought over a few pillows and other decorations from Snow's, the department store she worked at, that she thought would look good throughout the house. Isabella was more than happy to let Traci do whatever she wanted. She had such a gift for it, and though Isabella had a good sense for design, she had no ability to pull it all together the way Traci did.

"How are you feeling?" she asked Traci as she pulled up a stool next to her.

"Big." She laughed and patted her stomach. "I'm starting to really feel huge and they're moving around like crazy now. Feel right here." She grabbed Isabella's hand and placed it on her stomach where her hand had been. Isabella felt nothing at first and then she felt it, a faint flutter, and then something harder. A kick.

"That was pretty incredible," she said, and noticed Travis staring at her with a funny smile on his face. He mouthed the word "soon" and she blushed. Traci happened to catch it, too, and chuckled.

"My brother is dying to get you pregnant. I think then he'll finally be able to relax."

"What do you mean?"

"Just that he's been in love with you forever," she said.

"You knew?" Isabella was surprised.

"I'm the only one. It's a twin thing."

"Well, I'm not going anywhere. I'm madly in love with your brother, too," she assured Traci.

"I know. It's pretty obvious to me. I'm really happy for the both of you." Traci gave her a hug and Isabella felt misty-eyed again. She'd been so emotional lately.

"Is your sister here?" Traci asked, looking around the room.

"No, she went back to Ireland a few weeks ago, to do more research and spend some time with Ian. She'll be back for the wedding, though, and will hopefully bring Ian, too."

"Maybe it will be a double-wedding?" Traci teased, and Isabella laughed.

"I've only met him once, but they do seem pretty smitten with each other. It wouldn't surprise me at all if it goes in that direction."

"What about Anna?" Traci asked as she walked towards them.

"What about her?"

"Is she dating anyone?"

Isabella frowned. "No. It's been almost a year-and-a-half since her divorce. I've told her she needs to come out more with us."

"I'll have to keep my eyes and ears open for her. I feel like we should know someone for Anna."

"Me, too. Beauville is so small, though. I feel like we know everyone too and there's no one left."

"Someone will turn up, and Bozeman isn't far. That opens up more possibilities."

"Why do I feel like you two have been talking about me?" Anna asked as she sat in an empty chair next to Traci.

"We were just saying how pretty you looked," Traci said.

"And how we need to find someone for you," Isabella admitted.

Anna sighed. "I appreciate the idea, but the thought of dating and getting out there again just makes me tired."

"Don't even worry about it," Traci advised her. "Just be open and do things you enjoy. They say you meet people when you least expect it, and as my mother used to say, make sure you look good whenever you go out, just in case."

Anna laughed. "That's good advice. Seems like the only time I do run into people I know is when I don't want to be seen, when I'm wearing old sweats or something. I will definitely keep that in mind."

She turned to Isabella. "I am just so thrilled for you, both of you." Travis

WALKED OVER THEN AND PUT HIS ARM AROUND ISABELLA. "I'VE never seen you so relaxed and happy."

"Thank you," Isabella said, and Travis added, "Good friends, family and love. What more do we need?"

"I'll drink to that," said Uncle Jim.

LATER THAT EVENING, WHEN EVERYONE HAD LEFT, ISABELLA went upstairs to use the bathroom and to change into her favorite comfy sweats. When she came back downstairs, Travis was sitting by the fire in the living room, watching TV and patting Jolene, who was curled up behind him on the back of the sofa. The cozy scene brought tears to her eyes again and she smiled to herself. At least now she knew why she'd been feeling so emotional lately.

Isabella settled next to Travis and pulled a soft throw over her legs. She had something to tell him.

"So, I guess I sort of told a white lie to Uncle Jim earlier," she said.

Travis looked confused. "What are you talking about?"

"Well, I didn't know at the time, but I started wondering when I was talking to Traci and realized that every little thing seems to make my eyes water lately. I just took a pregnancy test now, and it was positive."

Travis looked stunned. "Are you serious? We're going to have a baby?"

Isabella smiled. "At least one, anyway."

"How far along do you think you are?"

"Not far at all, but I'll make an appointment for next week and find out for sure. It's still early enough that hopefully it won't be too noticeable at the wedding."

"It doesn't matter if it is. I want everyone to know." Travis pulled her in and gave her a kiss.

"You're happy about this?" Isabella teased. Travis looked like he'd just won the lottery.

"Happy doesn't begin to cover it. I love you and I already love this baby."

"Maybe we can move the wedding up a bit?" Isabella wondered out loud.

"Tomorrow's not soon enough for me," Travis said as he pulled her to him and leaned in for a kiss.

"Have I mentioned that I love you?" Isabella ran her hand through his hair and sighed with happiness.

"That's something I'll never get sick of hearing." Travis grinned and those dancing dimples that she loved so much were the last things she saw before he kissed her.

~The End~

Author's Note: The proposal scene is courtesy of my good friend, Dana Finnegan. This series was inspired by Dana, when she moved to Bozeman, MT and fell in love with Chuck, a great guy she met in a local kayak club.

Up next is Match-Making in Montana, which is Anna's story.

SNEAK PEEK—NASHVILLE DREAMS

Laura's story, Nashville Dreams is a standalone novel— a saga about soul mates torn apart by amnesia and an evil billionaire with political ambitions. It's also a story about finding your true passion in love and life and following wherever it may lead...

Laura Scott patted her stomach and snuggled against her boyfriend, Cole Dawson. He tightened his arms around her and kissed her forehead gently as the warm, Charleston breeze danced over them. They were in their favorite spot, sprawled on the soft grass and leaning against the big old oak tree that overlooked a shallow pond, where a family of swans floated by. They'd come here on their first official date, two years ago, after getting ice cream cones and strolling through the park. The old tree had beckoned to them and gave a bit of privacy as they watched people walking along the water's edge.

Laura sighed with happiness. On this sunny afternoon, a week after graduating from high school, she suddenly felt very adult and ready to take on the world, and was relatively sure of her place in it. She glanced down at the modest diamond engagement ring she was wearing. Cole had given it to her a few days ago, and she couldn't stop staring at it. Her mother had been thrilled, and relieved, considering.

Laura hadn't ever really worried though, except for the initial day of panic when she learned the news and couldn't understand how it had happened, as they'd been so careful. Her doctor explained that the antibiotics she'd been taking for an ear infection had canceled out the birth control. She and Cole had already talked about getting married though and having children. She loved kids and he said he wanted a houseful of them, though neither one of them had expected to get started quite so early. It did change their plans a bit.

"I'll have to let Montana State know that I won't be attending after all. Hopefully Clemson will still let me in." Laura was planning to be an elementary school teacher.

"Of course they will. They did accept you. And if it's too late for this year, you can do community college and then start up fresh in the Fall."

"That could work. How do you think your father will take it? Do you want me to come with you?" Laura noticed a muscle clench in Cole's jaw and knew that he was dreading the conversation that he needed to have.

"He's back tonight, and we're having dinner at the club. I thought that might be a good place to tell him. He can't go too crazy if we're out in public, especially there."

Cole's father could be intimidating, and although she'd offered to join Cole, to support him, Laura was actually glad that she wouldn't be there. As sure as Cole was about getting married, she knew that his father was going to give him a hard time about it. Dalton Dawson was a big deal in Charleston. No one knew exactly how much he was worth, but it was rumored to be multiple billions.

He was a real estate developer with holdings all over the country. He was smart, driven, and Laura suspected, a bit ruthless. She didn't particularly care for the man. He and Cole couldn't be more different. Where his father was hard and ambitious, Cole was sensitive, caring and creative. His dream was to be a country music artist.

Laura suspected that Cole took after his mother who had once been a singer too. She'd never had the chance to meet her, as she'd died a year before she and Cole started dating, but he spoke of her often and had played some of her old recordings for Laura. She had a lovely voice. She had softened his father's edges and they'd been madly in love. When she died, six months after being diagnosed with lung cancer, his father changed.

He threw himself into work even more and recently found a new focus. He was determined to be the next Governor of South Carolina. Which was another reason he wasn't going to like their news. Dalton Dawson was a staunch Republican and conservative family values was a key part of his platform. His son knocking up a teenager who lived in a trailer park wasn't going to go over well.

"He'll just have to deal with it. People have babies all the time, and at least we're getting married. I told him over a month ago that I was going to ask you to marry me, so that won't be a surprise."

Laura chuckled. "He tried to talk you out of it, I imagine?"

"Well, yes. He said we're too young for one thing." Cole looked like he was going to say something else, then thought better of it and Laura imagined that his father had shared a few more reasons as to why their getting married wasn't a good idea. He didn't think she was good enough.

Cole reached into his pocket and drew out a swiss army knife. He opened it and then smiled at Laura as he turned around and found the heart he'd carved into the old tree on their first date. It simply said Laura and Cole and the simple gesture had endeared him to her then. They'd seen each other almost every day since.

Cole didn't care that she lived in a trailer park, and he liked her mother. Laura and Cole were best friends, and she couldn't imagine not having him in her life. She watched with curiosity as he carved something below their names. When he was done, he leaned back so she could see. It was a single word, in small letters so it could fit into the heart and it said, 'Forever'.

"There is nothing that my father can say, that will change my mind. We are getting married, as soon as possible. And then we're going to start the rest of our life together."

Laura's mother was sitting on the patio smoking a cigarette when Cole dropped her off. He waved goodbye as Laura joined her mother and pulled up a chair. Technically where they lived was considered a mobile home, but there were no wheels. They were manufactured homes, modest, but well-kept and Laura had never minded living there. It was other people that seemed to mind, catty girls mostly, and as her mother had reminded her more than once, if they had a problem with where she lived, that said more about their own issues.

As of a few years ago, her mother had paid off the mortgage and now owned her home free and clear. She was a tiny woman, just over five feet tall and about a hundred pounds. Unlike Laura's hair, which was long, fine and stick straight, her mother's was the same sandy blonde shade, but short and wavy and she didn't have to do a thing except run a comb through it.

She also had blue eyes, a cute nose and an easy smile. She'd been beautiful when she was younger and in Laura's opinion, still was. She looked tired today though. She worked as a waitress at a family restaurant and must have worked the lunch shift as she was still in her uniform and had a glass of chablis by her side. She enjoyed her wine and often had several glasses at the end of a long day.

"Has Cole told his father yet?" Her mother seemed worried. She knew as well as Laura did that Dalton Dawson was not going to be happy to hear this news.

"He's been out of town. They're talking tonight, at the club."

Her mother took a sip of wine and then a long drag on her cigarette.

"You don't have to get married you know. If it's going to cause problems. You and the baby can stay here. There's room for all of us."

Laura reached out and squeezed her mother's arm. She knew that she really wouldn't mind having them stay. In fact, she'd probably love it. Laura's mother had been about her age when she found herself unexpectedly pregnant as well. Like Laura, she'd been in love and Richard, Laura's father, had been in love with her too.

They'd married and everything had been wonderful, until a few years later when her father hurt his back on a construction site and became hooked on painkillers. He died in his sleep one night after an accidental overdose, which her mother blamed herself for and never really got over. Richard had been the love of her life, and though she occasionally went on a date, her heart wasn't in it. Laura worried that it might be hard for her when she moved out, and she was glad that Cole had agreed to stay in Charleston, so they would still be close to their families.

"Thank you. I think it will be okay though. Cole is determined to get married, with or without his father's blessing."

Cole met his father at the club. His father's office was right around the corner and Cole was relieved to take his own car and not have to deal with with the black mood his father was sure to be in. The Breville Country Club was the most exclusive club in Charleston. His father was a regular there and often held business meetings in the bar or at dinner.

Cole parked his old Volvo sedan in the parking lot and made his way into the club. It was an ostentatious place and he'd never felt comfortable there. His father loved it. A marble floored entry-way opened into the lounge, which had plush royal blue carpet, black leather seats and polished dark wood. Cole found his father at the bar, chatting with several friends over a freshly poured martini. He smiled when he saw Cole.

"Right on time. What can I get you to drink?"

"I'll have a beer, an IPA on draft if they have it."

Mandy, the bartender, winked at Cole as she slid a freshly poured beer toward him.

"Nice to see you, Cole. It's been awhile," she said with a smile. Mandy had just graduated too and Cole had known her for years. He hadn't been to the club in a long time. He used to golf more but in recent months it hadn't been on his mind much.

"Thanks. It's been too long."

"You ready to sit down? Our table is ready whenever you are," his father said as his two friends paid their tab and left.

"Sure." As ready as he'd ever be. His father led them to a corner table by a window that faced out onto the course. Two menus were already there and the other two settings had been removed. They sat and his father took a long sip of his drink. He looked like he was about to say something, then opened his menu instead.

A moment later, Edwin, the waiter that had been at the club for as long as Cole could remember, came by to tell them the specials and take their orders. They both got the same thing they always did, sirloin strip steaks and a loaded baked potato. Once Edwin left, his father turned to him.

"All right. Out with it. What's so important that we're having this conversation here?"

Cole took a deep breath. His father was still dressed for success in a rich tweed blazer and red silk tie and he exuded power. He was tan too, from spending the last week in the Bahamas. Although he was in his early fifties, he had only a dusting of gray around his temples, which was mostly hidden by the gel he used on his thick, black hair.

"It's Laura. You know how I told you a month or so ago that we wanted to get married?"

His father scowled and reached for a hot roll as Edwin set a bread basket on the table with a tub of butter.

"I thought we decided that it was too soon for you to be thinking marriage? Better to wait until you are out of college. See if you're still even together then?" He slathered butter on his bread, took a bite and then added, "Maybe you'll find someone more …..appropriate?"

Cole clenched his fist and fought the urge to smash something. He had to look away from the sneer on his father's face. When he spoke about Laura it was as if he was thinking of something distasteful and it disgusted Cole.

"Dad, there is no one who is more appropriate for me than Laura."

"You say that now. You have to think of your future, and where you are going and choose a partner that will be an asset. Bernie Thirwood told me just the other day that he'd be happy to have you join them when you finish law school."

Cole sighed. "I've never said I would go to law school. I don't think I want to be a lawyer."

"It's an excellent choice for you. It will give you options.

Open doors for other things. If you major in tax that would be really helpful for the business. If you eventually decide to come on board."

"I don't see myself following in your footsteps Dad. I'm sorry, but real estate development doesn't interest me."

"Well, what does then? You're not still thinking foolish thoughts about Nashville and country music?"

"I am. That's my dream." Cole lifted his chin and met his father's eyes. "I'm good too. People have said so."

His father laughed. "Who said that? Your girlfriend? And you wonder why I don't think she is a good choice for you. You need to be practical, son. Play around with music all you want, as a hobby. But you need a good education, a business degree at least, followed by law school."

"I'll think about it, law school that is. I am in for the business program." Cole figured it might not be a bad idea to make his father seem like he was going along with his recommendations. To calm him before they headed into stormy waters.

"Good. And I'm glad you decided on Clemson. Now what's so important?"

Their meals arrived and Cole waited a moment, letting his father cut into his steak and take his first bite before proceeding to ruin his meal.

"Dad, we're going through with getting married, sometime over the next few weeks and then we'll get a place together near Clemson."

"Why would you do that? I thought you said she was going out of state? Washington or Montana?"

He cut another bite of steak and Cole did the same, and was just about to explain when his father set his fork down.

"She's pregnant?" His voice was cold, his eyes stormy as he glared at his son.

Cole nodded.

"This isn't good, for any of us."

Cole nodded again.

His father furrowed his brow and Cole knew he was scrambling for a solution, a way out.

"You know I'm considering a run for governor? People are telling me the time is right. I think it might be, too. But this isn't good. This is the kind of thing that won't reflect well on us. She lives in a trailer park for god's sake."

"It's not like that. Not really. Where she lives is nice and neat."

"You can put lipstick on a pig, but everyone knows it's still a pig. It's a trailer park, no matter what else you want to call it."

"Fine, but still, there's nothing wrong with it."

"And she's pregnant and now you want to marry her. You should be starting your college years unencumbered, not with a baby on the way." He paused for a moment and then asked, "Will she consider an abortion?" He brightened as he said it and Cole cringed. His father was such a hypocrite.

"I didn't think you approved of that? That you were pro-life?"

"Well, yes, I am. Of course I am. But sometimes hard decisions must be made, for extenuating circumstances. As long as it's handled discreetly, no one needs to know."

"She doesn't want an abortion. Neither do I."

They finished their meals in silence. His father ordered another martini and checked emails on his phone while Cole gladly accepted another beer. When their plates were cleared, his father turned to him with an offer.

"If she agrees to get an abortion, I will pay for her to attend that school in Montana. I think that would be the best for everyone. If you're still wanting to be together after you finish college, then so be it. But I think it would be a huge mistake for the two of you to have this baby. You'll run this by her, let her decide?"

Cole felt his meal threaten to come back up.

"She won't agree. I know her."

"That may be. But you'll ask her?"

"Fine. I'll ask her. But I wouldn't get your hopes up."

"I think it's really sweet that Cole wants to come with you," Laura's mother said as they pulled up to the Dawson mansion. Laura had spoken to Cole briefly earlier that day. He'd called and confirmed that he still wanted to come for the doctor visit. Her doctor was going to do the first ultrasound and they were both excited to see their baby. Cole had sounded tense on the phone though. She'd asked him how the dinner had gone the night before and all he'd said was that it had gone about as well as he'd expected and he'd fill her in later.

Laura jumped out to walk to the front door and get Cole, while her mother waited in the car. Since it was the middle of the afternoon, she knew she wasn't likely to run into his father, but she was still nervous as she approached the front door. It was an intimidating house. It was huge, and they had live-in help. When Laura knocked on the door, it was opened by Sergio, their Brazilian butler. He broke into a wide smile when he saw Laura.

"Come on in, I'll tell Cole that you're here."

Laura stepped inside and waited in the foyer while Sergio went to get Cole. She glanced around, at the sleek marble floors and soaring ceilings with elegant artwork on the softly shaded walls. His house was gorgeous and felt more like a museum than a home to her. But she never said anything to Cole, as it was all he knew, and it was beautiful. Just not what she would ever want. She heard footsteps and looked up to see him bounding down the stairs, a smile on his face.

"You're in a good mood," she said as he pulled her in for a quick kiss.

"I'm in a great mood. We're going to meet our baby for the first time. How cool is that?" Laura relaxed a bit as they walked outside and toward the car, where her mother was smiling and waving at them. She'd trusted that Cole wouldn't let his father get to him, to change their plans, but still the worry had been there. Dalton Dawson was a powerful, and ruthless man and she knew that he had never approved of her.

Laura got back into the front seat and Cole settled into the back. They both buckled up as her mother pulled out of the driveway and onto the main road. The doctor's office was just a few miles away.

"Thanks for coming to get me," Cole said to her mother.

"Of course. I'm thrilled that you wanted to be there for Laura."

Traffic was light, and they were running a few minutes ahead of schedule. The last thing that any of them remembered was a large SUV that was going much too fast. It swerved into the opposite lane—and there was no time for her mother to react, to get out of the way. The SUV hit them head on, and in the span of just a few seconds, everything changed.

———

Hope you enjoyed this sneak peek of Nashville Dreams!

ABOUT THE AUTHOR

Pamela M. Kelley is a USA Today and Wall Street Journal bestselling author of women's fiction, family sagas, and suspense. Readers often describe her books as feel-good reads with people you'd want as friends.

She lives in a historic seaside town near Cape Cod and just south of Boston. She has always been an avid reader of women's fiction, romance, mysteries, thrillers and cook books. There's also a good chance you might get hungry when you read her books as she is a foodie, and occasionally shares a recipe or two.

Let's connect!

www.pamelakelley.com
pam@pamelakelley.com

Made in the USA
Monee, IL
01 March 2021